ATTIC CANDLELIGHT TALES: LARGE PRINT EDITIONS

Ember Flames

Novelist Artist Love Bro Bones

Illustrations by Novelist Artist Love Bro Bones

First edition 2024

CONTENTS

PROLOGUE

In the quiet of a stormy night, William stumbled upon a small attic room filled with books. Looking around at the scattered volumes and creaky wooden floorboards, he felt a sense of wonder.

But the book on the pedestal in the center of the room truly captured his heart. Its well-worn pages and yellowed edges spoke of a history rich in meaning and emotions. William felt drawn to the book's stories and characters and spent countless hours lost in their world.

As time passed, William's love for the book only grew stronger. It became a constant companion, a source of comfort and joy during even the most challenging times. And though he is said to have passed away, the spirit of William lives on in the magic of that night.

For those whose power of a good book has touched, William's story is a reminder of the transformative power of literature. It speaks to the empathy and understanding found in the pages of a beloved book and the comfort and solace it can bring to our lives.

PART 1
LEGEND WAS
BORN

CHAPTER ONE

BROTHER AND SISTER

In ancient times, long before the town of Marland took shape, there existed a majestic kingdom called Appledill, home to diverse beings. This kingdom was ruled by a wise and just monarch named King Adam, who was not just a ruler of humans but also had dominion over a host of fairy tale characters. The kingdom of Appledill was a place where magic and reality intertwined, and both the human and fairy tale subjects coexisted peacefully.

King Adam was born to Queen Snow White and King Charles White, making him a prince of royal lineage. He was known for his wisdom, kindness, and fair rule, which earned him the love and respect of his subjects. King Adam had a twin sister named Eve White, who was equally beautiful and kind-hearted. Together, they ruled the kingdom gracefully and compassionfully, ensuring all their subjects lived in peace and harmony.

The kingdom of Appledill was a place of wonder and magic, where fairy tale creatures like unicorns, dragons, and fairies roamed free. It was a land of enchantment, where the impossible was made possible, and stories came to life. King Adam and his sister Eve were loved and revered by all their subjects, who looked up to them as shining examples of good leadership. While the kingdom of Appledill may have faded into oblivion, the stories of King Adam and his sister Eve lived on, inspiring generations to come.

However, as time passed, Adam and Eve's parents fell ill and eventually passed away, leaving Adam as the sole ruler of Appledill. This sudden turn of events left Eve feeling angry and resentful. She believed their shared blood, a unique blend of fairytale and mortal genetics, was a curse rather than a gift.

Eve's animosity towards fairytale characters intensified, and she despised them. She believed that fairytales were merely fictional creations harbored in the minds of men and stories they had heard, coming to life through their imagination. As a result, Eve desired to divide the kingdom and establish two separate domains, one for the mortals and one for fairytale characters. In her view, this separation was necessary to maintain order and prevent conflicts from combining the two realms.

Despite Eve's resentment, it is clear that her brother Adam possessed a unique gift that many viewed as precious and invaluable. His ability to serve both humans and fairytale characters with equal care and attention was something that many believed would pave the way for a harmonious and prosperous future where both worlds could coexist peacefully.

As the new king, Adam faced the daunting challenge of bringing the two factions together under his rule. He was determined to maintain the delicate balance established during his parents' reign, ensuring that humans and fairytale characters were treated fairly, justly, and respectfully.

However, his efforts to reconcile with his once-beloved sister, Eve, were met with conflict, and eventually, they parted ways. Eve's departure left her struggling with the loss of

their parents, and her result-
ing madness led her to venture
deep into the dark and foreboding Cinder Woods.

Meanwhile, Adam had married
a princess of the Seas, and together, they had a child named
Lilly. Adam was determined to
provide his daughter with the
best possible training and guid-
ance so she could one day
become the next ruler of Appledill.

However, something unexpected happened. Eve, the sister
Adam had once loved and cher-

ished, was overtaken by madness. The once-gentle and nurturing spirit within her was consumed by darkness, and she became a wicked witch with dark and terrible powers. It's hard to imagine how difficult it must have been for Adam to see his sister change beyond recognition and abandon her innocent ways.

Adam was an exceptional man who faced many challenges and difficulties but never gave up on his quest for unity, equality, and justice for all. His empathy and compassion for humans and fairytale characters were remarkable, making him a beloved leader who inspired everyone around him.

As time passed, Adam began to experience a shift in his emotions. The loss of his wife had a profound impact on him, and he found himself developing a deep sense of empathy towards his sister. His heart ached for her, and he was determined to find her, even though he was unaware of the danger that awaited him.

Unfortunately, Adam's search

for Eve would be a grave mistake. Unbeknownst to him, his beloved sister had been driven into madness and transformed into a darkened heart witch with immense powers. When Adam finally discovered the truth, it was too late. The once-loving bond between them had been shattered, replaced by a deep sense of betrayal and regret.

With his once beloved sister now lost to him, Adam was left to deal with the pain and grief he had experienced. It was a difficult time for him, but he found comfort in the support of his loyal subjects and in the memories of the love he had shared with his wife and child.

Despite his heartbreak, Adam refused to give up on Eve. He knew that her descent into madness did not reflect her true nature. He held on to the hope that there was still a glimmer of light within her that had once been filled with darkness. This knowledge drove him to continue searching for answers, hoping that one day, he might find a way to bring his sister back into the fold and mend the broken bond that once existed between them.

Amidst the picturesque kingdom of Appledill, Lilly grew into a charming and beautiful young lady. Every step she took was graceful and elegant, captivating everyone around her. Her charm and beauty left everyone in awe. In stark contrast, Eve watched from afar with resentment and disdain, her heart consumed by the darkness that had engulfed her.

Eve, also known as Mother Gothel, has harbored

deep-seated anger and resentment towards fairy tales. Whenever she heard stories of love, kindness, and happy endings, her frustration and jealousy boiled over; as she grew older, she plotted revenge against her brother's kingdom, using her magic to transform into the Evil Fairy Godmother.

In her secluded hideout at the old cottage of the Seven Dwarfs, Eve gathered her powers and began crafting her sinister plan. She was fueled by her twisted desires and an insatiable need for control. After months of preparation, she set out to lure Lilly into her trap with a letter promising a life-changing surprise.

The letter was Eve's master-piece, a carefully crafted work of art designed to manipu-late Lilly. However, it inadver-tently revealed the depths of her wickedness, exposing Eve's true nature as Mother Gothel, the Evil Fairy Godmother. The letter reflected her twisted de-sires and her relentless need for control, which only intensi-fied her frustrations and jeal-ousy.

Eve's grand plan for Lilly's birthday was her ultimate revenge. She eagerly awaited Lilly's arrival, consumed by the darkness that had taken over her, and with a wave of her wand, Eve transformed into a mythical fairy with robes of white and a staff of darkness. The crow perched on her shoulder, and the darkness followed her every move.

When Lilly arrived, she was greeted by Mother Gothel in her new form, shocked to see the wickedness in her eyes. Lilly was trapped and baited by the Evil Fairy Godmother's dark magic, turning her into a frog. Lilly felt bewildered and trapped as she watched Eve disappear into the darkness.

The peaceful and enchanted garden, with its tranquil pond and seven charming dwarf cottages, provided a serene sanctuary for the figure. As she looked upon her reflection in the water, her heart may have been heavy with sorrow, but she never gave up hope for a better tomorrow.

Once a grand and noble ruler,

Prince Lilly had been cursed and transformed into a small green frog. Despite her current state, she remained steadfast in her belief that she would one day return to her rightful form and kingdom. With its beauty and serenity, the garden provided a refuge and tranquillity, a reminder to never give up hope, even in the darkest times.

.

CHAPTER TWO

DRUNKEN KNIGHTS CURSED

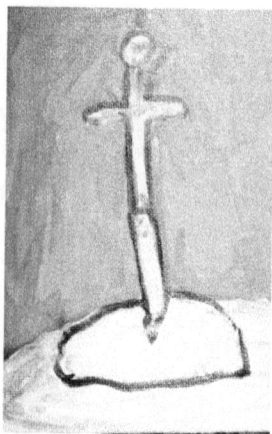

In this world of magic and curses, the fate of Appledill and Eve lies in the balance, caught in the middle of a tumultuous battle. Adama's daughter is trapped in a hidden garden of seven dwarfs, transformed into a frog for eternity, waiting for true love's kiss to break the spell. However, many have failed in their attempts to claim this gift, leaving her fate uncertain.

Appledill's life is in danger, as she is at risk of falling into the hands of Eve or Mother Gothel, who will stop at nothing to gain control. Eve and Appledill's fate depends on Lily's actions, whose curse has left her with the ability to find freedom only with the truest of hearts.

A young prince, his brave general, and a crooked magician lead an army of drunken knights into battle, guided by King Adam himself. They fight against the wrathful Mother Gothel, once known as Eve, who has succumbed to wickedness and betrayed her family. King Adam is heartbroken but holds onto the hope that there is still life in his sister and that she can be redeemed.

As the battle rages on, the kingdom spirals into madness and destruction. The fight between wits and time leaves the world questioning humanity's fate and the enduring power of fairy tales amidst the chaos. The outcome of this conflict will determine not only the fate of Appledill and Eve but also the fate of the world itself.

King Adam watches helplessly as the world around him spirals into chaos and destruction, and the lives of his loved ones hang in the balance. The young prince, his general, and the crooked magician fight bravely and cunningly, leading their army of drunken knights into the fray. Each move they make is critical, as the kingdom's fate rests on their shoulders.

The battle is fierce, and the stakes are high. The kingdom's fate hangs in the balance, with Appledill's life and Eve's redemption at stake. The young prince and his allies fight with empathy and compassion, knowing that the cost of victory may be too high. They understand that the unfolding events may forever change the kingdom and work tirelessly to ensure that as much good as possible can come from this struggle.

As the conflict reaches its climax, there is a sense of sadness and loss, hope, and renewal. No matter what happens, the young prince and his allies know they have done everything possible to protect those they love and ensure that the kingdom remains a place of justice, compassion, and empathy.

Amid a tumultuous conflict, the kingdom's fate and humanity hung in the balance. The enduring power of fairy tales held the promise of salvation, with true love's kiss offering the possibility of breaking Appledill's eternal curse. Meanwhile, the fate of Eve, a key player in the struggle, remained uncertain, with the possibility of redemption or downfall hanging in the balance.

Despite the high stakes and ongoing turmoil, the people fighting for the kingdom's survival remained resolute. They knew that the outcome of this conflict would determine not only the kingdom's fate but the entire world. They held fast to hope through all the uncertainty and adversity, believing that a peaceful resolution was possible.

As the conflict raged on, whether man and fairy tales could peacefully coexist lingered in the air. It was a daunting challenge, but those fighting for the kingdom refused to give up. They drew strength from the idea that someday, somehow, a resolution could be reached to end the never-ending battle between good and evil.

And so, amidst the turmoil, they pressed on, driven by the hope that their efforts would ultimately bring peace and a brighter future.

In this epic tale, the fate of the realms hangs in the balance as Arthur, a fearless warrior, his trusted general, and a cunning magician, embark on a perilous journey to defeat the evil Mother Gothel and save their world from chaos. The story takes us on a thrilling adventure as the group faces numerous challenges, including escaping the clutches of time and battling against their enemy's wicked heart.

Despite the daunting obstacles, the group persists, using their wits and skills to overcome their adversaries. Through thievery, swords, and drunken magic, they fight valiantly to protect their land and people. However, they soon realize that their efforts may not be enough and must seek a new strategy to defeat their powerful enemy.

General Charming, the commander officer of the Drunken Knights, devises a daring plan to strike a deal with Mother Gothel to sanctify his bloodline. However, the cost of this deal is a curse that will plague his family for generations to come, with his son, Prince Charming, bearing the ultimate consequences. Despite this grave risk, the group continues to fight, with Prince Charming falling in love with a maiden girl and marrying her in true love.

Unfortunately, the curse on the Charming bloodline takes effect, leading to a tragic end to their happiness. On their child's sixteenth birthday, she pricks her finger on a spinning wheel and falls into a deep sleep for a hundred years, only to awaken with true love's kiss. But the curse also causes her to turn into dust and ashes, signaling the fairy tale's end.

As the story progresses, Mother Gothel becomes more powerful, posing an even more significant threat to the group's efforts. She uses her dark magic powers to whip away the Drunken Knights' memories, killing Prince Arthur. Meanwhile, General Charming and the crooked magician seal themselves inside a bubble, bringing the story's fairy tale realm and characters back into their books and sealing the fate of the Charmings, the cursed of the Charming bloodline.

Despite the setbacks, hope is still alive, with the creation of a lock buckle book, the key to bringing back the kingdom and its stories. The book can unleash the magic of a fair child's imagination, sought by the crooked magician in a prophecy he had in lighted candle embers flames. The attic's homes are filled with classic fairy tale books, eagerly waiting to be discovered by curious children.

As the story concludes, King Adam hides, and General Commander Charming has his first-born son, Prince Charming. However, the curse begins to sprout, and the magician seals Appledill and its people around the gothic stone wall, preventing time from moving. But as fate would have it, the time comes when Lilly rises again, becoming queen and re-awakening Appledill and its people. Thus, the town of Maryland is born, and Magichion's son, William White, is cast into a storybook, signaling the beginning of a new prophecy.

CHAPTER THREE

HIDDEN ATTIC

Ten years ago, a young boy named William White was exploring his family's large, old home on a warm summer's day. William was a curious and adventurous child, always eager to discover something new. As he wandered through the house, he noticed a creaky old ladder that led up to the attic space.

Without hesitation, William climbed the ladder, feeling a sense of excitement and anticipation building within him. As he reached the top of the ladder, he was face to face with a wooden clasp door that seemed to be calling out to him. He slowly unclasped the door with trembling hands, revealing a dark, dusty room filled with old books.

William's eyes widened in wonder as he stepped further into the room, taking in the sight before him. The books were stacked haphazardly on shelves that lined the walls, each one appearing to be older than the next. He couldn't help but feel a sense of awe and reverence for the knowledge and history contained within those pages.

William stepped into the dimly lit room, his eyes scanning the shelves of books that stood tall and imposing, their spines cracked and their pages yellowed with age. The scent of old parchment and leather bindings filled his nostrils, and he felt a sense of excitement and anticipation as he began to explore this treasure trove of knowledge and adventure.

As he walked deeper into the room, he noticed an old wooden chair, its surface worn and faded from years of use. It faced a large round glass window that offered a view of the storm raging outside. The sound of raindrops tapping against the windowpane echoed through the room, adding to the sense of mystery and intrigue.

As he searched through the books, his fingers brushed against the rough textures of the bindings and the smooth surfaces of the pages. Suddenly, his eyes fell upon a leather-bound book with a golden strap that glittered in the dim light. He hesitated momentarily, his mind warning him against opening it, but his childhood sense of wonder and imagination got the better of him, and he reached for the book.

The pages crackled with age as he opened the book, and a faint aroma of old ink wafted up to his nose. As he read, he felt a sense of wonder and awe, the magic of the story coming to life in his mind. The night flew by as he lost himself in the adventure, the storm outside raging on. Lightning flashed, illuminating the room in a bright white light as thunder boomed, adding to the story's drama.

When he finally looked up, he saw the sun rising, its warm rays streaming through the window. He felt a sense of deep satisfaction, knowing he had experienced something truly magical. As he placed the book back on the pedestal, he felt a sense of reverence for the story it contained.

Suddenly, he was surrounded by sparkling fairy dust, the tiny particles covering his skin. He felt a strange sensation as if his soul separated from his body. The book had opened a split in time, and as his soul entered the pages, it also transferred itself into the dust.

Once inside the story, he watched history unfold, lurking as a dusty shadow. The tale of the White family and everything that had come before flowed before his eyes, and he felt a sense of wonder at the unfolding drama. He saw the characters come to life, their struggles and triumphs playing out before him in vivid detail. The adventure had just begun, and he was eager to see where it would take him next.

CHAPTER FOUR

UNKNOWN TALES

Life can be entire of moments that seem to exist outside of time, where memories are frozen in timelessness and reality is blurred with fiction. These precious moments are like jewels that sparkle with an ethereal light that illuminates our souls, reminding us of the beauty that exists in this world.

In the stillness of the night, a single flame flickers inside a candle, casting a warm glow that illuminates the dusty attics of the townsfolk. The soft light serves as a reminder that even in the darkest times, there is always a glimmer of hope guiding us home.

As we lose ourselves in the pages of a story, we realize that the flames in the hour-glass of time mark the beginning of eternity. Each turn of the page inspires our imagination and fills our hearts with an indescribable sense of wonder. The characters become natural, and we feel their struggles and triumphs as if they were our own. The line between dream and reality blurs, and we wonder if there is more to this story than what we can see on the page.

We become lost in the tale, the words becoming a portal to a different world. The air is thick with the scent of adventure, and we feel a sense of antici-pation as we turn each page. The story becomes a journey, a trek through the depths of our imagination.

Finally, we come to a locked door, and we can't help but wonder what secrets lie beyond it. The door is old, the wood rough and weathered. We can feel the weight of history and mystery surrounding it. It's as if the door is a metaphor for the challenges we face and obstacles we must overcome to reach our goals. But we are not alone in this journey. We are here together, supporting each other every step of the way. And as we unlock the door and step through, we know that whatever lies beyond, we will face it together.

As each night begins to rise with a single light of a candle into the depth of the burning embers, summoning the unknown reaches of mysteries of your house containing inside trap doors of an attic, keys unlocking the truth or lies, so what do you most desire is the question you ask yourself and your wishes may come true.

In the small town of Maryland, the Gothic walls surrounding the town are more than just physical barriers. The children of Maryland embody a world of fantasy and wonder that offers a respite from the monotony of everyday life. The Gothic walls provide a glimpse of a world beyond their imagination, where anything is possible, and magic is real.

Walking through the town square makes it easy to sense the town's relaxed and unhurried pace of life. The clock tower at the center serves as a reminder that time seems to stand still in this town. This is a source of contentment and peace for the townsfolk, but for the children, it's a source of endless fascination and wonder.

In their dreams, the children are transported to a world beyond their wildest dreams, where they can be whoever they want and go wherever they please. They imagine themselves as brave knights, fighting dragons and rescuing damsels in distress, or as princesses trapped in towers, waiting to be rescued by their valiant knights.

The Gothic walls surrounding the town symbolize the town's rich history and the power of the human imagination. They inspire the children to dream big, to believe in magic, and never to stop exploring the world around them. In this town, time may stand still, but the spirit of adventure and wonder that resides within the hearts of the townsfolk continues to burn brightly, lighting the way for generations to come.

"Let's take a moment to embrace the magic of childhood and the limitless possibilities of imagination that it brings. We should empathize with the children in Maryland, recognizing the importance of cherishing and fostering their creativity and encouraging them to continue dreaming and exploring the world around them.

Seeing the adults in Maryland

losing their sense of wonder and joy over time is disheartening. Their face appear dull, and their surroundings are colorless, reflecting the loss of enthusiasm that once shone so brightly. They have become too absorbed in their work, forgetting the value of play, imagination, and laughter.

Maryland feels lost, as though it has forgotten how to enjoy life's simple pleasures and the beauty that surrounds it. We understand how frustrating and disappointing it can be to feel trapped in a life devoid of vibrancy and inspiration.

Even the happiness that the children bring with their growing minds can't seem to reawaken the colors of the world or the reality they live in. Time stands still in this town, leaving a sense of stagnation and disappointment.

But, with a bit of light, the community can be revitalized. We must empathize with the adults and inspire them to reconnect with their youth's joy and wonder, rekindle the fire of their imagination, and see the world with fresh eyes. By doing so, Maryland can once again flourish, bursting with the world's colors and its people's happiness."

CHAPTER FIVE

THE WHITE APPLE

In the heart of Maryland's town square, a single tree stood tall amidst a wild storm, bearing a single white crispy apple. The tree was surrounded by a beautiful garden that had taken root in the town square, with the clock tower standing tall at its center. The townspeople were known as the Life Fruit, and their beauty and aroma were legendary.

Nobody knew where the tree came from or who planted it, but it had become a part of the town's folklore, bringing the townspeople together and giving them a sense of pride and belonging. The tree's legend had been passed down from generation to generation, becoming a symbol of hope and magic for the people of Maryland.

Despite the mystery surrounding the tree, it reminded the townspeople that there was always hope, even in the toughest of times. The tree had weathered the storm and continued to grow, inspiring the townspeople to be resilient and never give up in the face of adversity.

The townspeople felt a deep connection to the tree as if it were part of them. They knew the tree had faced many challenges, just like they had, and it had emerged more robust and beautiful than ever before. The tree was a testament to the human spirit, inspiring the townspeople to be kind, compassionate, and empathetic towards one another.

For the people of Maryland, the tree was not just a tree but a symbol of their shared humanity, and it reminded them to treat one another with kindness and respect, no matter what challenges they faced.

On a calm autumn day, a small hooded boy approached the mythical tree in the town center. He snuck into the tree's gated and fenced garden and plucked a white, crispy apple. As he took a bite, the thundercloud roared into the crystal blue skies, and a moment of silence fell over the town of Maryland. After a few seconds, the town clock tower began to tick again.

The hooded boy stood there, announcing, "I'm William White, the boy of stories and dreams!" The boy from the dream realm unlocked the keys to Maryland's past, present, and future, becoming the un-locker of their lands and stories.

As thunder crackled and lightning struck the ground, the boy disappeared, leaving a lingering question: "Do you seek an answer to be found behind the locked door?" The people of Maryland knew that the boy had opened up a new world of possibilities for them. They could feel the weight of their struggles and marveled at the boy's bravery and determination.

At that moment, they realized that they, too, could unlock the secrets of their own lives. They could overcome their fears and doubts, and they could embrace their own unique stories. They knew the power to change their lives was within them, and they felt a sense of empathy for the boy who had shown them the way.

PART 2 THE ATTIC TALES

CHAPTER SIX

FOOL'S KINGDOM

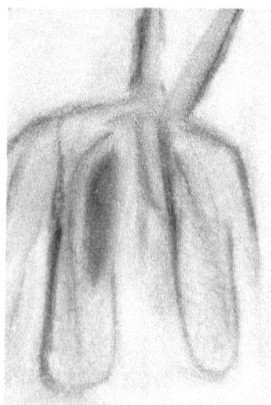

The past has ended, and in its wake, history has

been written and passed down through the ages.

These stories have been told countless times, yet they may only be considered fiction as they may not be entirely accurate. It's a curious thing to understand something without experiencing it yourself. You may ponder it repeatedly, but it's not until you drift off into a deep sleep that you can truly immerse yourself in the stories you've heard. As you close your eyes, you may find yourself lost in a world of imagination where anything is possible.

Do these dreams hold any truth, or are they just a figment of your imagination? The answer may lie within your consciousness, and it's up to you to interpret what these dreams may mean. Regardless of their meaning, your dreams are a unique and personal experience only you can understand. They are a testament to the power of the human mind and its ability to create entire worlds from the depths of our imagination.

The town of Maryland was filled with people going about their daily tasks, seemingly oblivious to the dark and stormy sky above. The Gothic stone walls surrounding the city only added to the feeling of melancholy that permeated the air. Despite the gloom, the town's children saw the world with wonder and imagination. The gift of candlelights brought a much-needed spark of life to the gray and colorless world, and their young minds were filled with awe and delight.

However, the magic that the children experienced came at a cost. The potential for evil to twist all that was good was ever-present, and the consequences could be dire. It was a small price to pay for the joy and wonder that the children brought to the town, but it was a price nonetheless.

As the town went about daily, unaware of the small event that would significantly impact their lives, one could not help but feel empathy for them. The people of Maryland lived with carefree abandon, seemingly oblivious to the storm clouds that hung above. But bene, on the surface, a sense of resilience was truly admirable. Despite their challenges, the people of Maryland remained optimistic, and their strength of character was truly inspiring.

One night, a boy named Benny Harrison crept toward a dusty stairway leading to the attic of his home.

Books were waiting for him, waiting to be read. As he climbed onto that old dusty chair, which sat so casually by the round window, he sat down to read one.

Benny found solace in the cozy armchair surrounded by neatly stacked piles of books. As he picked up the worn-out copy, he noticed the soft ember glow emanating from a nearby candle illuminating the pages with a warm, comforting light. Benny opened the book and began reading, unaware that the story contained magic.

The tale of "Jack and the Beanstalk" takes him on a journey through a far-off land filled with adventure and bravery. Benny was captivated by the story and felt a deep empathy for the poor boy named Jack, who was sent to the market to sell the family cow to provide for his sick mother.

As Benny read on, he found himself engrossed in the story, eagerly following the twists and turns as Jack faced numerous challenges and triumphed over them. He felt the pain and hardship that Jack experienced and the determination and resilience that kept him going.

As the night wore on, Benny fell into a deep sleep, clutching the book in his lap. The townspeople of Maryland awoke to find a strange and wondrous sight. A gigantic cornstalk grew from the clock tower, its long tendrils reaching the heavens.

The folks of Maryland gathered around the enormous plant, marveling at its size and strangeness. They felt a sense of wonder, awe, and empathy for the characters in the story and their challenges. The magic of the book had touched their hearts, and they felt a deep connection to the characters and the journey they had gone through.

The story of Jack and Benny's journey through the book reminds us that we all face challenges in life and can find strength and inspiration in the stories of others. By empathizing with the characters and their struggles, we can better appreciate life's journey and the resilience it takes to overcome adversity.

Unknown to anyone, there was a screech from a window. He wasn't known or discovered—this screech came from a girl named Amy.

Amy is the youngest of two children in the Harrison family. Her older brother, Benny Harrison, slept in the attic this morning. Their parents were known Booksellers in the town, and all the children went to their shops for their stories.

She had always admired her brother since he was incredibly wise and very good at reading books filled with story tales. Benny wasn't in bed when she looked for him there, so she knew where he was. She also knew whether parents kept their remarkable treasure hoard of books.

As Amy walked up the attic staircase to see what her brother was up to, she heard the stairs creaking. But when she reached the attic, she found her brother asleep in the chair. However, as she approached him, she realized something much darker was happening. Her heart sank as she touched his cold body and realized that he had passed away. Overcome with grief, Amy made a wish while holding her brother's limp body, wishing that he could be reborn.

Meanwhile, the townsfolk stared at an overgrown corn stalk when they noticed something strange. A young boy emerged from the clouds and climbed down the branch, carrying what appeared to be a sack full of goodies.

As Little Jack entered the town square, he caught the townspeople's attention with his small bag of gold that he claimed had fallen from the clouds. As he walked through Maryland, he began distributing the gold to the people, bringing hope to those in need.

Among the people who received the gift of gold were the Harrison family, who had recently suffered a significant loss. Although they were still grieving, they received the gift with gratitude, hoping it would comfort their shattered hearts.

As Amy, one of the family members, received her share of the gold, she looked at Little Jack and felt a sudden jolt of recognition. She knew in her heart that he was her brother reborn. The realization hit her hard, and she felt many emotions wash over her.

At that moment, she understood the true meaning of the book her brother had possessed - "To gain a life, one must lose a life." Benny had traded his old life for this new one as Jack. The gift of gold he had brought with him symbolized renewal and hope for the townspeople. In their grief, they had found solace; in Little Jack, they found a reason to hope again.

CHAPTER
SEVEN

WONDERLAND
COTTAGE

As you delve into the pages of this captivating book, allow me to take you on a journey of empathy and understanding. Picture a vast farmland, isolated from the bustling town square, surrounded by dense woods. Beyond it lies a hidden cottage, home to Timmy and Nibble, two twins with unique personalities. Nibble, in particular, has a bright and imaginative mind that shines with pure beauty. Her story is one of hope and inspiration, reminding us that we all have the power to create our magical worlds. Let her journey fill you with empathy and compassion and inspire you to see the beauty in the world around you. Allow yourself to be transported to a place of wonder and under-standing where anything is pos-sible.

The story of Nibble and Lit-tle Timmy is one of heartache and loss but also resilience and hope. Losing their parents was an unimaginable tragedy, but they have found comfort in each other's company and the love and care of their dear grandma.

Exploring the small Attic of their grandma's cottage has become a source of joy and inspiration for Nibble and Little Timmy as they discover the treasures of books she has stashed away. These books have become a precious escape for them, a way to lose themselves in worlds of adventure, mystery, and friendship.

Their story is a poignant reminder of the power of imagination to heal and guide us through difficult times. Despite the pain of loss, Nibble and Little Timmy's imaginative spirits shine, lighting the way forward for them. May we all be inspired by their story and find solace in the love and support of those around us.

As the night falls and the rest of the house drifts off to sleep, Nibbles, the compassionate and empathetic soul, seeks solace in the rough and bundled Attic. She finds comfort in her favorite book, Alice's Wonderland, and becomes lost in a world of fantasy and magic.

As she reads, Nibbles is reminded of the power of imagination and the magic within each of us. She reflects on the stories of her childhood and can't help but wonder about the types of childhoods others had, where magic was confirmed in their world. She imagines life's endless possibilities if the impossible is possible and feels a sense of understanding for those who have faced obstacles.

As the creatures of the night begin to stir, Nibbles feels a sense of empathy for those who may be struggling in the darkness. She thinks of those who may be feeling lost or alone and wishes she could offer them the same solace she found in her book.

As the morning sun shines through the window, Nibbles wakes up with a smile, feeling grateful for the escape that her book has provided. She hurries out of the Attic, eager to face the day and to offer kindness and compassion to those around her. The memories of her magical journey are still fresh in her mind; she feels inspired to spread hope and positivity in the world, one small act of kindness at a time.

The kitchen was cozy, with a large table in the center and a blazing oven on the far side.

As the protagonist watched her grandma arrange the china plates, she noticed the strained smile on her grandma's face. "Hello, dear; I see you found grannies' old books. But you might be starving by now, reading and dreaming all night."

Nibble felt a sense of empathy towards her grandma. Even though she was uneasy, she watched her grandma move around the kitchen with a gentle grace. As the trapdoor creaked open, Nibble felt sad when she saw Timmy in the birdcage. She could see the fear in his eyes, making her heart ache. She knew that she had to act quickly to help her friend. Nibble's experience taught her the importance of being empathetic to others, even in the most challenging situations. She realized empathy could go a long way in making a difference in someone's life. She could find inner strength and courage even in the most challenging conditions.

As she stood there, her mind went blank, and her body froze in shock. She had never seen something like this before. Her grandmother smiled at her with a glint in her eye, taking pleasure in her granddaughter's reaction. Then, with a deep, boisterous laugh, she complimented the meal they had just finished. "Delicious, Hun," she said. "Sweet and tender and plump and juicy, the best meal for breakfast." Suddenly, Nibble, the woman's granddaughter, sprang into action. She lunged forward, knocking down the birdcage holding her brother, and then shoved her grandma into the oven. The woman watched in horror as the flames began to consume her flesh, turning it into embers. Nibble felt no regret for her actions; she believed it was the only way to protect herself and her twin brother. The twins, still in shock, walked through the dark woods to Maryland, wondering what horrors awaited them in the future.

Timmy followed his sister, Nibble, down the winding path, deep in thought about the strange events of the morning. He was still trying to make sense of it all. They saw something that caught their attention as they approached their neighbor's house. It was a tea party, but not just any tea party. The decorations and atmosphere were identical to Mad Hatter's mad tea party from Alice's Adventures in Wonderland. The twins were surprised but also curious to find out more. They wondered if they were even allowed to join the fun.

Being the bolder of the two, Nibble stepped forward and knocked on the door. A moment later, it opened, and the twins were greeted by a sight that took their breath away. The table was overflowing with delicious treats and various mismatched cups and saucers. The chairs were all different shapes and sizes, and the room was decorated with colorful bunting and whimsical knick-knacks. Mr. Hatter sat at the head of the table, his wide grin welcoming them.

The twins approached the table hesitantly, unsure if they were welcome. Mr. Hatter, noticing their apprehension, beckoned them to join in the fun. They sat down, and the tea party began. The tea was sweet, and the treats were delicious, but the conversation was the most memorable. Mr. Hatter regaled the twins with his incredible stories, and they listened intently, captivated by his every word.

As the tea party ended, the twins couldn't help but feel a sense of affection for Mr. Hatter. He seemed to feel the same way and made a special connection with the lost children. From that day on, Mr. Hatter became a beloved figure in their lives and decided to adopt them as his own. The twins left the tea party feeling grateful and excited for the adventures ahead.

CHAPTER EIGHT

COOKIES CRUMBLE

O nce the bravest and most respected warriors, the Lost Drunken Knights found themselves drinking at a local pub, seemingly forgotten by the rest of the world. Their adventure, heroism, and magic stories filled the air as they shared their drinks around a stone table. Each knight had a story to share, and their tales were told with a sense of longing for a past that had been lost.

Despite the doubts of many patrons, these knights refused to let go of the memories of their youth. They spoke sadly about the battles they had fought and the friends they had lost along the way. The night was filled with laughter, but it was also tinged with a sense of melancholy.

As the full moon illuminated the knights, their faces shone with pride and regret. They had once been great, but now they were forgotten by all but themselves. The Lost Drunken Knights may have been lost in time, but they will never forget their sacrifices.

The Lost Drunken Knights' stories were a poignant reminder of the human condition, that even the strongest warriors could be vulnerable and that time could be a harsh mistress. The patrons at the pub listened with rapt attention, enthralled by the knights' tales. They felt empathy for the knights, recognizing that their struggles and fears were their reflections.

Upstairs, the baker's family owned a part of the pub, and beside it was the bakery renowned throughout the town for its delicious gingerbread. Two young boys often sneaked into the shop to listen to the stories on the other side of the wall. On a starry night, after the baker's wife had put their youngest son to bed, a warm glow emanated from a candle, illuminating the room. The elder son read from his collection of books, planning to read two before calling it a night.

The first book was an epic tale of King Arthur and his Knights of the Round Table, while the second was a childhood favorite about the Gingerbread Man. Although the stories were different, they both contained elements of magic and wonder. Arthur's adventures were awe-inspiring, while the Gingerbread Man's story was relatable, as the warm scent of baking filled the room.

As he read passionately, the town clock tower chimed twelve, and something magical seemed to awaken in the room. The stories came alive in his imagination, and he felt he could see the knights and the Gingerbread Man come to life before him. Finishing the book, John blew out the candle flame, set down his round glasses, and crawled into bed, his mind still filled with the images and emotions evoked by the stories.

The clock's ringing shook the leaves of the corn stalk, creating a sense of adventure and danger. The drunken Knights stumbled out of the bar, oblivious to the storm, wobbling their way forward. As they stumbled down the gravel road, they saw shadows moving in the forest. Suddenly, the shadows took on the shape of figures that seemed strangely familiar. The Knights were filled with profound emotion, and they recognized these figures as old friends from deep within their memories.

However, their drunken state did not serve them well, and one of the Knights tripped over a log that had fallen on the road, sending him tumbling to the ground. The others followed, tripping over each other in their drunken stupor. As they lay motionless, a group of riders approached them. King Arthur revealed himself, ready to fight, and the Knights were confused and disorientated.

But the crooked man with them held up his wand, and with a swish of its powers, he restored their lost memories. Suddenly, the Knights knew what they had to do. They fought valiantly against the giant, determined to restore peace to the land.

As the battle ended, the Knights knew that this was a night they would never forget. They had accomplished something great, and they had done it together. They empathized with each other, realizing they had been lost in their drunkenness and were lucky to have been saved by their friends.

As the untold forces of magic began to manifest, the previously monochromatic environs surrounding them underwent a peculiar transformation. Previously dull and lifeless, colorless objects were now imbued with a spectacular intensity of color. This newfound vibrancy was perhaps a foretaste of the wonders that awaited them.

The perceptible change in the environment was gradual but undeniable. The once faded and dreary landscape now teemed with various hues and vivid shades, producing a breathtaking visual spectacle. Flowers, which had hitherto been wilted and lifeless, suddenly sprang to life, bursting forth with renewed vitality as if drawing sustenance from the magical energy that flowed in the air.

The sky, which a uniform grayness had previously dominated, now erupted into a kaleidoscope of colors, as if a rainbow had exploded into a million tiny fragments, scattering them across the sky. Even the rocks and stones that littered the ground were infused with a newfound vitality, seemingly reinvigorated by the very essence of the magic that permeated the air.

As they beheld the sight before them in awe, they could not help but ponder whether this was merely a glimpse of the extraordinary sights that awaited them in the realm. If this was just the beginning, the possibilities ahead were endless, and the adventure awaited them promised to be nothing short of exceptional.

CHAPTER
NINE

WARDROBE
ATTIC

On the square's outskirts lies a simple townhouse with a tower of stone bricks.

This tower townhouse was a marvelous sight in the town of Maryland. It was the home where the Whittling family dwelled. Mr. Miller Whittling was the town folks' wheat flour supplier, and Ms. Rose Whittling was a well-known tailor who made the finest clothes.

And most importantly, they had a bright young daughter named Apple.

Apple was a shy, quiet girl who had no friends. She spent most of her free time exploring the nearby woods that border her family farm. Other times, she delighted herself by climbing the tippy top of the tower. She liked to call the cupboard Attic; there, she always felt more at home. It was a cozy space with a wardrobe, a pile of books, and a small, round window.

Often, Apple would sit in front of the window, reading her books while the sun shone through. In her eyes, books could take her on many beautiful adventures. They allowed her to journey through the world of imagination.

On one particularly breezy day, Apple explored the woods and collected wild strawberries. As she skipped along the dirt pathway, she began to find herself in a deeper part of the forest where she had never been before.

There, she came across a white-picked fence. Behind this fence was a gorgeous garden. Curiosity getting the better of her, she pressed forward. As she journeyed closer in, she spotted an adorable table full of chinaware containing teapots, teacups, and plates full of delicate pastries ready to be eaten.

Looking past it all, her eyes were drawn to a white house with rows of vines holding pink flowers. Now, she became even more curious, taking it upon herself to see who lives in such incredible beauty.

Stepping across the stone path and reaching the doorstep, Apple paused slightly before the door. She went to quietly knock on the red door when the door abruptly opened. On the other side of the door stood a short man who wore a fine robe and decorated top hat.

He looked up at Apple with a tender, cheery smile and bowed slightly. "Hello, little miss, and what do I owe the pleasure of this visit from such a young girl at my door? " people stood there for a second, unsure what to say. "W l, I just came by wanting to say

hello. And Uhm... to ask what that charming tea table is doing outside?" "The kind fellow smiled and spoke again.""Well every, that is my tea party table! Every day at noon, it is where I have an unbirthday birthday party." He then looked Apple up and down and raised a single eyebrow. "Would you like to join two children and me?" Apple thought a moment, rubbing her chin. It couldn't do much harm. And I do like the tea table. And the garden. Apple then smiled and said," Yes, I would like to join you."

.   On that note, Apple met and celebrated an unbirthday party with her new friends: Mr. Hatter, Timmy, and Nibble. They were a joyous bunch who knew how to pass the time. Deciding she should be polite, she invited them all to her home for dinner. Mr. Hatter declined, as he had matters to attend to, but he encouraged the two little ones to go.

Later in the evening, Nibble and Timmy join Apple and her family for supper.

Once done eating, the three friends raced up the tower's stairway. As they entered the cardboard attic, Nibble gasped when she saw the piles of books. Tim y, awestruck, just gazed around.

Apple could read the expression on her new friend's

face. She could tell they wanted to sit down, dig inside a book, and get lost in its pages. Nib le then looked up at Apple's face with a smile. In a soft voice, she said almost to herself, "Wow, you're a bookworm just like me, that's so cool... Can I read your books? "Ap le laughed in reply. "Of course you can, my friend. "

The night was edging on the horizon while the three friends sat around the window. Apple struck a match, then lit the wick of the candle. It is here where the storytelling brings forth the magic.

As the embers burned and flames danced, Apple began reading the telling tale of Narnia aloud. The two had their listening ears on as they listened to each word. The s ory sang around the room, fluttering in tiny ember dust like that fairy dust.

Embers spiraled as night was in full swing. Behind the children, the wardrobe began to glow. Little Timmy noticed it at first, but eventually, they all wiggled with excitement. Unable to contain her curiosity, Apple hurried up towards the wardrobe, letting the book fall from her hands. She swung open the doors. The light that poured in was so intense she had to shield her eyes until they adjusted.

The glow came from a magical sight of wonders, a new realm to explore. Nibble, who watched with curiosity, followed shortly behind Apple. She's back at the open wardrobe doors, her eyes wide as her words fall out of "Wonderland."

With no worries, Apple bravely spoke, "Well, what are we

staring at? Let us set off on an adventure through and out of Wonderland." That moment, their adventure began, and the three friends stepped into the wardrobe that led into Wonderland. They left the world behind with no regret.

Stepping out of the wardrobe, they were thrown into the world of Wonderland. They didn't know it then, but they were beginning the adventure of a lifetime. Then, as they looked back one last time, they noticed that the wooden doors behind them had closed. It was unknown to them how or when they would return home again. The cold reality was that they were lost in a world of fiction and genuine madness.

After some discussion, the three friends agreed they would spend as much time exploring before it ended as all stories do. That is precisely what they did, going along the paths surrounded by wonder as if they were Alice herself. Even the friends came across a chatty and annoying singing flower field | The flares led to the land of, but something didn't feel right. Up ad, the colors of the winds were dark, and they could feel they were going into the grim gloom. Death was to awaken the dawn with silent whispers. The v id pages echoed as the three friends walked into the black shadows, ruins of lands that had once claimed the in-between beauty of past, present, and future.

What has happened to the world of Wonderland? Could madness have broken out in this once-loved childhood tale?

A distinguished grin of a crooked smile creeped out,

and then two glistening eyes blinked open from the dark woods. They lowed in the dark, and the smile showed no regrets. Sudde ly, it danced out of sight, almost like an illusion, a figment of imagination.

It had stopped them in their tracks, for they felt the forest was playing mind tricks on them. Then, without a second thought, the same characteristic grin appeared again. This time, when it came, the eyes and mouth were outlined in shadow that framed a familiar face. Unbelievably, it began to grin an even bigger smile. Finally realizing who it was, Apple and Nibble laughed and then looked into the eyes of the figure. Deed, it was the mischievous cat known as Chester. Longer afraid, they pushed onward into the dark woods. The clues echoed as they completed the puzzle that was the pages of this world.

In need of a change of scenery, they left the deep crevices of the forest that the shadows had overtaken. Before long, they came across a familiar white picket fence that led into the depths of a garden entwined with a crumbing table. The party table was still set up with ceramic tea cups and china plates coated with thick dust. Inside were crumbs from old tarts and spiders that had made their homes there. s the friends left, they shut the white gate with a feeling of melancholy in the air. That is when they noticed a sign on the gate that read, "Here we honor the old Mad Hatter and the laughing memories he gave us. May he rest in peace."

Alarmed,   questionable thoughts raced into the minds of the three friends. They thought, what does it mean that the Mad Hatter is dead? An impossible answer came about, but how impossible could it be? They questioned it for every reason.

Seemingly reading each other's minds, they spoke aloud all at once. " could the story be alive but stuck in a loop? How does it play out if Mad Hatter is dead? Could he be dead in this world but alive in theirs? could it be that part of the story lives in our world?" These questions haunted them as the friends then stumbled upon the white Rabbit running about in his red coat. He was scrambling in his pockets, then looked at his watch, to which he exclaimed, "I'm late, oh I'm Late!"

Nibble, Apple, and Timmy look at each other, curious to see how the story has been rewritten. Yearning for answers, they followed the White Rabbit Clues hinted about as they came upon a garden of red roses. Here, two dumb twins greeted them. Before they could spin silly little tales, a small woman dressed in a red robe drew near.

In a kind, sweet voice, she welcomed them. For she had foreseen their coming, information she had gotten from the wise caterpillar. She invited them to join her for tea. While the three of them sipped their tea, they were told a tale of a forgotten past

CHAPTER
TEN

HIDDEN
DOORWAY

The Whittling family, who resided in their charming town tower townhouse in Maryland, were once happy, filled with love and laughter. However, that all changed when they lost their dear child, Apple. The devastating loss has left Mr. and Mrs. Whittling heartbroken and struggling to understand their grief.

Since the tragedy, Mr. Whittling, who was once a proud and loving father, has become distant and withdrawn. He spends most days staring out the window, lost in thought. Mrs. Whittling, who was once a vibrant and cheerful mother, has now become a shadow of her former self. She spends most of her days in her child's room, surrounded by Apple's belongings, trying to find solace in her memories.

Once filled with warmth and joy, the town tower townhouse now echoes with the silence of loss. The absence of their dear child, Apple, has left an unfillable void in the hearts of the Whittling family. They are now trying to find a way to pick up the pieces and move forward, but the road ahead seems long and uncertain.

The Whittling family found a curious object inside their wardrobe on a bright sunny day. As they touched the object's tip, they felt a strange sensation coursing through their bodies, like a magic power was awakening. Suddenly, the wardrobe started shaking and creaking as if something powerful was trying to break out from within. The object's tip started glowing with a bright light that grew stronger by the second, illuminating the room with a dazzling brilliance.

The family watched in awe as

the magic unfolded before their eyes. They could feel a sense of wonder and excitement they had never experienced before, knowing that something extraordinary was happening, and they were grateful to be a part of it. At that moment, they felt their inner souls awakening with the power of magic and knew that their lives would never be the same again.

However, suddenly, the hay roof that covered the top of the brick stone tower townhouse sparkled and burst outward, raining down a shower of debris and rubble that fell to the ground. The towering townhouse that had once stood tall was now nothing more than a pile of ruins, with only the wardrobe remaining unscathed.

As the heavy wooden doors of the old farmhouse swung open, a strange and otherworldly army emerged from the Whittling farmlands. The townsfolk gathered around, their eyes widening in disbelief at the bizarre sight before them.

The army was led by a towering stack of red cards, each one made from blood-red hearts. On top of the stack, a person with an enormous head and an ethereal, flowing red dress made from the same hearts sat perched like a queen on her throne. The townsfolk stared in awe as the cards began to move, shuffling and shifting as if alive.

As the army passed through the doorway, they were hit by a sudden burst of spotlights, illuminating their strange and mesmerizing appearance. The townsfolk were entranced as if transported to a different world. The army moved with a peculiar, otherworldly grace as if they were characters from a storybook brought to life.

As the sun set on the quaint town of Maryland, unexpected guests arrived in the form of three young children. Nibble, Timmy, and Apple found themselves in Wonderland, where they spent an unknown amount of time. When they returned, they were no longer the same; they had become the Queen of Hearts' sons and daughters and the looking glass's fair protectors.

As they settled into their new roles, they learned of their duty to reclaim the keys and master the Mad Hatter, now known as Mr. Hatter, who had become lost in their realm. Mr. Hatter had become forgetful, and his memories were lost in a spell that needed to be broken. Only Nibble, Timmy, and Apple could free him from this spell and restore his memories.

With determination in their hearts, the three friends set out on their mission, knowing that the fate of Maryland rested on their success.

It was as if Wonderland had come to their town, and the shadows of different realms had spoken. The people of Maryland felt as if they had come home to Alic's world, but their faith in their world was now tied into knots. They were unsure what to make of this surreal and magical experience, but they knew their world would never be the same again.

"This moment served as a reminder that magic can manifest itself in various forms and can transform lives in ways we least expect. Even in the face of seemingly impossible situations, there exists a spark of magic within us that can guide us towards the right path. The Whittling family and the townspeople learned that by embracing the mysteries of the world, we can uncover an inner power that we never knew existed."

Afraid or not, they could not think about their fate or their reality. The two worlds had joined, and life carried its way in the storyteller's dreams and childhood destiny.

Could a book's characters and fairytales be our fate? What does it all mean?

CHAPTER
ELEVEN

GRANDMA'S
KITCHEN

Nestled on the edge of
a sprawling forest, just
a few miles east of town,

a charming and picturesque townhouse exudes tranquility and serenity. The townhouse was previously an inn known to the locals as the Granny Shoe Inn due to its unique and captivating exterior that resembles an overgrown shoe. The inn was a bustling hub of activity, with travelers from all over the region stopping by to experience its genuine charm and appeal.

The inn's owner, Ginger, was a kind-hearted and gracious older woman, well-loved by all who knew her. Ginger was famous for her delectable apple pies, considered a local delicacy. She spent countless hours in the kitchen, mixing and kneading the dough, slicing and dicing the apples, and baking the pies perfectly.

The aroma of freshly baked pies wafted through the air, drawing people from all over the town to the inn. Ginger was always busy baking and eating her special apple pies, which she considered her life's work. Her secret recipe was guarded fiercely, and she often spent hours experimenting with new ingredients and techniques to create the perfect pie.

Despite her busy schedule, Ginger always had time for her guests, who were treated like family. She would sit with them and chat, sharing stories and laughter, while they enjoyed her mouth-watering apple pies. The Granny Shoe Inn was a place of warmth and hospitality, a haven of peace and tranquility, where people came to forget their worries and enjoy life's simple pleasures.

Little Plum, a girl living in the deep woods, had a sweet tooth, and Granny Ginger's Shoe Inn was a place of comfort for her. She loved taking long walks along the yellow brick path, enjoying the gentle rustle of leaves and the scent of ripe apples in the orchard. As she entered the inn, she was greeted by Whisker Boots, the tabby cat who made himself comfortable on the front porch, offering her a friendly welcome.

The familiar aroma of cinnamon and apples filled the air as she hung up her coat and boots. Following the scent, she went to the kitchen, where Granny Ginger prepared her signature dish. Little Plum settled onto a corner stool, watching as her grandmother worked her magic gracefully and skillfully.

The Shoe Inn held another secret treasure: a tiny crawl space at the very top of the inn. Its highest peak held a collection of classic children's books, which Granny Ginger had carefully collected over the years. Little Plum would spend hours lost in the pages of her favorite novels, transported to magical lands and enchanted forests.

In the heartwarming and cozy atmosphere of Granny Ginger's Shoe Inn, Little Plum found a sense of solace and comfort. Wrapped in woolen blankets in the tiny crawlspace, she followed the story of The Wizard of Oz, imagining the magic that could exist in the edging air. The warm glow of the candlestick and the sound of the storm raging outside provided a sense of familiarity and safety.

Suddenly, a lightning bolt struck the top of the Shoe Inn, and Plum was swept away into the stormy, star-lined skies, holding onto her beloved cat, Whisker Boots. Amid the chaos, Plum's heart raced with uncertainty and fear. She wondered where the winds would take her and if she would ever see her grandmother Ginger or taste those delectable pies again.

Despite the confusion and the unknown, Plum held onto her sense of wonder and imagination. As she looked down upon the bright desert, her heart filled with hope and inspiration. She knew that despite adversity, there was always a way to persevere and find joy.

Ultimately, Plum's journey reminds us that no matter how difficult things may seem, we can always find comfort and inspiration in the world around us. The Shoe Inn may have been just a tiny space, but for Plum, it was a place of empathy and understanding where she found hope and solace.

The night was stormy, and Plum felt like a child again, laughing as she looked at the sights before her. She was swept away by the magic of it all, recalling the silly but marvelous book she had read and feeling grateful to be at this sky party. She let her mind wander and imagined the desert below her as the Land of Oz, feeling like she was living in a fantasy. It was much like the book she had read, where Dorothy and Toto flew over the windy breezes in their house. But Plum was whisked away by a rough draft with an umbrella and the company of Whisker Boots, who carried her through the clouds in time.

She arrived at the clearing and saw farmers' towns scattered among corn and wheat fields. A passionate yellow brick road connected the tiny blue dome homes, and tiny people were gathered around the farm-like towns, singing joyfully. Plum was mesmerized by the sight and wanted to experience their happiness firsthand. But before she could, the wind swooped her up and away, causing her to land in a chimney of one of the houses. The chimney was narrow, and Plum slid down it with a bump before entering a tiny old house that appeared empty. The broken windows and dusty old furniture immediately caught her attention, and she realized that this was Dorothy's cottage. Excitedly, Her eyes widened, and she exclaimed, "I'm in Oz!"

But her excitement was short-lived as the walls around her crumbled and collapsed, causing Plum to be blamed for the destruction. She was confused and scared, but fortunately, Ozma agreed to be her friend. From that day forward, Ozma and Ozling became great friends of Plum herself, and they explored the magical land of Oz together.

CHAPTER TWELVE

WILLOWING TEARS

Granny Ginger sat on the old wooden bench outside her tiny, cozy, shoe-shaped inn, nestled deep within a dense forest. The inn's crack in the wall allowed a sliver of light to filter in, illuminating the bench and the forest floor beneath it. Ginger gazed up at the sky, her eyes scanning each twinkling star beyond the star's line, marking each one off in her mind as she counted them individually.

As she counted, she made a wish on every shooting star that streaked across the sky, hoping that the light would reveal a path or sign in the moonshine of the day. She longed for her beloved granddaughter, Little Plum, to appear before her and request special apple pies.

But life had taken a cruel turn when a storm blew away Little Plum and her daring Whiskers Boots. Since then, Ginger's adored granddaughter had been missing, leaving her heart shattered into a million pieces. She tried to imagine the world through Plum's eyes, but the memories only brought her more pain.

As the days passed, even the once-praised pies Ginger made

with love and care became a shapeless blob, mirroring her shattered heart and thoughts. Even the passing travelers who used to stop by and praise her pies couldn't make her proud of them anymore. Everything around her seemed to have lost its sweetness, and Ginger felt alone and broken.

Yet, amid the darkness, Ginger's glimmer of hope remained. She continued to count the twinkling stars, making wishes on every shooting star, hoping that one day, her beloved granddaughter would return and everything would be sweet again. She could picture Plum's smiling face and hear her sweet voice requesting special apple pies.

As she sat there, lost in her thoughts, Ginger realized that the twinkling stars were like little beacons of hope in the darkness. They reminded her that even in the darkest times, a spark of light could still lead her out of the darkness. She knew that as long as she kept counting the stars and making wishes on every shooting star, her hope and love would shine brighter.

The devastating loss of Willow and her collection of children's books had left us reeling with grief and struggling to come to terms with the memories that lingered on. But for Ginger, those books were more than just a source of comfort - they were a lifeline, a place of sanctuary where she could retreat from the world and immerse herself in the magic of the stories.

The tiny attic at the top of her

Shoe Inn had become Ginger's cocoon, a cozy refuge where she could lose herself in the joy and wonder of the books she had accumulated over the years. The room was filled with the comforting scent of old books, and the flickering light of a single candle cast a warm glow over the pages.

One night, Ginger picked up a well-worn book and struck a match. The flame caught, casting a soft light over the pages. As she began to read, the story came to life before her eyes. The characters leaped off the page, their thoughts and emotions unfolding in vivid detail.

Ginger was no longer a spectator - she was part of the story. She felt the grass beneath her feet, smelled the sweet scent of wildflowers, and heard leaves rustling in the wind. The stars twinkled in the night sky, casting a soft glow over the pages, and she felt she could reach out and touch them.

Peek, one of her favorite characters, appeared, and Ginger felt a surge of emotion wash over her. She remembered the night Willow had arrived, bringing a sudden change in the weather and an upheaval in their lives. But at this moment, surrounded by the magic of the story, Ginger felt a sense of peace and joy that she wished could last forever.

Ginger's experiences remind us of the power of the written word and the beauty of the stories that speak to our hearts, offering us solace and comfort in the darkest times. It is a testament to the resilience of the human spirit and the power of hope to heal even the deepest wounds.

As the fierce storm howled outside, Ginger sat in her cozy armchair, wrapped in a soft blanket, and read a captivating book. The story was a thrilling adventure tale that transported her to a world of magic and wonder. She was lost in the pages when she noticed a change in the sky outside. The clouds, once a dull gray, were now a beautiful patchwork of grays, blues, and purples, and the stars shone brightly through the breaks in the clouds.

As the storm intensified, the rain grew heavier, tapping on the windowpanes like tiny fingertips. The pages of Ginger's book began to feel damp as the rain seeped through the cracks in the window, but she was too engrossed in the story to care. The sound of the rain mixed with the crackling of lightning and the rumble of thunder created an eerie atmosphere in the room, making Ginger feel like she was inside the story she was reading.

Despite the magic around her, Ginger couldn't help but feel a twinge of sadness as she re-membered her childhood. Her memories resurfaced, and she couldn't help but long for the simpler times when the world was full of magic and won-der. She tried to push those thoughts away and focus on her book when a sudden me-owing sound broke her concen-tration.

Ginger saw a little tornado swirling towards her, carrying a cat in boots and an umbrella. The cat, Little Plum, smiled and swung her umbrella in a friendly greeting. Little Plum's boots were soaked from the rain outside, and her fur was matted from the wind, but she seemed not to mind. She glided towards Ginger, her tail swishing back and forth, and meowed a greeting.

Ginger couldn't help but smile back at Little Plum, feeling a sense of warmth and joy she hadn't felt in a long time. Little Plum seemed to sense Ginger's feelings and curled on her lap, purring softly. Ginger stroked the cat's fur, grateful for the unexpected visitor on this stormy night. As she looked at Little Plum and felt the magic of the stormy night, she couldn't help but think that anything was possible. Perhaps the world was not so different from the one in her book.

CHAPTER
THIRTEEN

LETTERS IN
THE SKIES

The sky was dark and over-cast, with brooding clouds gathering overhead, signaling the imminent arrival of a thunderstorm. The atmosphere was electric with anticipation, and the first few raindrops fell gently, like small drumbeats against the leaves of the trees. Suddenly, the skies opened without warning, sending a torrential downpour that sent everyone scurrying for shelter.

But not everyone ran for cover. A group of people began twirling around the old Granny's Shoe Inn, their umbrellas held up to the sky as they danced in the rain. Each of them was unique, with their own stories etched on their faces. Some were young and carefree, with bright eyes and wide smiles, while others were old and wise, with wrinkles and weathered expressions that hinted at a lifetime of experiences.

As the rain continued to pour down soundly, the skies came down with raindrops of umbrellas from the skies holding hands of hands onto the grips of the umbrellas, where the group of people began to reveal themselves as characters from the fantastical world of storybooks. There was the Scare-crow, with his clever brains, the Tin Man, with his kind and caring heart, and the Coward-ly Lion, who had finally found his bravery. There was also a top-hatted Wizard of Oz, a childish girl who appeared to be Ozma, and finally, a woman in a bubble who could only be Glin-da the Good; all the leaders of O were gliding, joining the realm of humanity and fairytales.

It wasn't long before a new group of characters appeared in the sky, descending grace-fully towards the earth. These were the Ozlings, their umbrel-las in hand shimmering in the rain as they floated down to Maryland. Each was more magi-cal than the last, and their faces were full of wonder as they looked around at the unfamiliar world.

The humans welcomed them with open arms, eager to learn about their stories and share their own. The apple orchards surrounding Granny's Shoe Inn provided the perfect backdrop, with the scent of fresh ap-ples filling the air and the trees swaying in the wind. The sound of the rain and laughter echoed through the orchard, creating a symphony of happiness that would be remembered for years to come.

The two groups mingled and laughed as the rain continued to fall, sharing stories and swapping jokes. It was a moment of pure joy, where the lines between reality and fantasy blurred, and anything was possible. The Ozlings shared tales of their magical world, while the humans recounted their own stories of adventure and wonder. The rain slowly tapered off, leaving behind a glistening world, fresh and new after the storm.

In time, Ozma went to see her old friend, Miss Litlle Plum, who was living with her Granny Ginger of the Shoe Inn. Ozma arrived at the front door with a knock on the wooden door from it. Granny Ginger opened her doorway to her surprise to see the characters of her memories from her own favorite classic children's book standing in front of her. Granny Ginger looked far and wide, and her mind saw right. The character of Oz was just at her doorstep, just as she imagined.

Ozma, in childish ways, smiled in charming, inspiring words she spoke, " Good Morning; you must, Granny Ginger, that I heard so much about you from Miss Plum herself, for I'm a friend of hers and here in welcoming greeting to this wonderful world of Maryland with loyal proctors and leaders of the Ozling, in hopes be welcome to this realm for our new home so thought you and Miss Plum can give helping our magic to bring our lands together one simply harmony."

Over tea and pies and a touch of magic, the lands of Oz and the Ozling made their new home in Maryland.

The world changes even more with welcoming characters' storybook fate,

CHAPTER FOURTEEN

BLACKSMITH WORKBENCH

The town's local blacksmith is the home of the Captain's family, located in the heart of Maryland's Townsquare.

A small boy named Peter was one of the family's kind-hearted members. Peter was well-known for his entertaining puppet shows, which brought new life to those Sunday mornings after a long week.

People in Maryland referred to him as an artist or storyteller because of his wildest stories about his family and family before him and how they all started as pirates before becoming the bright, well-known blacksmith. The town had seen the best jewelry-making and serving and the finest silver-ware. Young Peter's eyes and mind brought him the childhood dream of creative imagination that any child could have.

It aided him in reading Grandpa Joe's books when he had the chance. Peter went to see his grandfather across Cherry Lane, on the outskirts of other town shops. It was sometimes difficult for him to get to Grandpa Joe's farm because Grandpa occasionally required assistance with the farm's animals.

Peter believed it was worth it for the days he would spend the night. He liked going up to the attic after work and discovering Grandpa Joe's old childhood books that he had when he was a young youth like him.

The story of Peter Pan was one of Peter's favorite books. This story alone convinced Peter that his ancestors were related to none other than Captain Hook himself. After Peter arrived at Grandpa Joe's farm, it was a stormy night.

To Peter's delight, he could stay with Grandpa Joe and

finish the Peter Pan story again. As the storm blew out the farm attic window, Peter sat in his grandfather's old chair, wrapped in wool blankets made by his grandmother Wendy, and read along with Peter Pan playing in his head. It was late, and the attic quickly became darker than usual.

Before calling it a night, Peter lit a small candle to finish reading. I appreciated each word calling out into the gentle breezes, as did the outside storm.

Like the ocean, the skies appeared in the book, with each

page turn and the intense, rolling scenes Peter read onward. Soon after, two clouds collided, causing a roar that startled Peter from his words on the page. Turn quickly towards the window before his eyes caught a glimpse of the skies that would forever change Peter's life. Like in his book, a pirate ship was in the mix of roaring clouds. In that split second, another flash appeared, but this was no ordinary lightning of blues and purples in rays of shine, a yellow glow sparkling the night skies like a shooting star lashing out into a million-to-one crystal. Peter jumped out of the chair he was sitting in and hopped down the attic stairs into the cold, chilly night in that split second. A ladder suddenly fell out of the sky, just enough for Peter to grab it. He dashed around the corner of his grandfather's farmhouse into the cornfield, hoping not to miss it.

He noticed the Captain's glances. Grandma Wendy astounded him.

A glorious figure emerges from the dark sword she held, complete with a feather-down coat and skull hat. A young boy stood proudly beside her, with younger little boys dressed in animal furs behind them. Captain Grandma Wendy, it could be, and the small boy standing next to her was, in fact, Peter.

Those who dance in circles like a tribe in the back are the lost boys of Neverland, the star island of the far north, a myth or legend that keeps coming back.

The table turned to   Grandma Wendy, who was looking at her late husband, Wendy; eventually, it came to be that she had to confront her old husband again, telling stories of Peter Pan and the Lost Boys and her lifetime struggle.

It was just a story for him, but he was taken aback when she vanished one night ago. When he opened the door away in the nights that followed, he was surprised to find a note from his wife and a child's book. He sat there, puzzled, staring and listening to his wife's tales of pirates, lost boys, and the death of Peter Pan.

Grandpa Joe's younger side returned to him as little bits of childminder drawings that blew in the wind as he stared back directly at his long-lost wife in little notes he took into his brain.

Wendy concluded her story by saying she had left the voice of the lost boy. It transported her back to Neverland with a single touch of her hand, her husband.

A single drop of magic resulted from it. Memories danced around the walls of the dining room.

Memories are long forgotten, and it is no longer necessary to bypass childhood, and a new life has been brought into Grandpa Joe's side of a forgotten and lost past.

He stared at a fairytale image of true magic releasing the man's bloodline. Details can reveal the truth you want to believe is absolute in the eyes of painting history,

but in Grandpa Joe's case, he was Captain James Hook's son, and his wife was Wendy Darling.

What about fairy tales that always have those hidden twists; in the collisions of thoughts,

Grandpa Joe felt deep within his bones what had been made clear in his forgotten childhood. Past. A childhood past that you wish you could never forget, but faith is no reason to bargain. Wendy looked into her husband's eyes briefly before speaking. "I left those many years ago from that lost boy's voice of a cry, and it was the breaking news of the death of Peter Pan and found a secret hidden in a jar of you being the son of Hook. The quest to find your Father led me to become lost as a pirate." Grandpa's face lit up with a smile and laughter now that he remembered why he found it at London's Clock Tower years ago. If you only believe in fairies, you will be able to fly.

CHAPTER FIFTEEN

TOADS STOOL MUSHROOMS

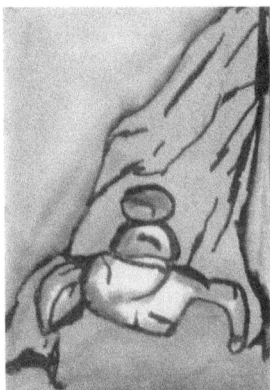

Little Henry Jr. is a charming and delightful ten-year-old

boy with a beaming smile and a twinkle in his bright eye. He lives in a cozy, rustic cottage with his kind-hearted stepfather and loving mother, nestled amidst the lush and verdant Huntsmen Woods. The woods are alive with chirping birds, rustling leaves, and babbling brooks flowing gently through the forest glades.

Henry is well-loved and respected in his community, affectionately known as Little Redwood. His nickname is derived from his vibrant and striking red hooded cape that he proudly wears. He is known for his gentle and compassionate nature and his willingness to lend a helping hand to anyone in need.

In his free time, Little Redwood indulges in his passion for baking. His petite kitchen is a wonderland of sweet delights, with the scent of freshly baked cookies, cakes, and pies wafting through the air. He takes great joy in sharing his culinary creations with his neighbors, often skipping happily through the woods with his basket full of delicious treats.

Little Redwood is a true gem of Huntsmen Woods, spreading joy and happiness wherever he goes. His challenges symbolize that The Huntsmen Woods was a place of beauty and heartache. Two groups had made their homes there, each with their own stories.

Henry and Redwood were two outsiders who had found comfort and acceptance among the Huntsmans. They were welcomed with open arms and shared food and stories with the community. Robin, the hunters' leader, had taken Henry under his wing, teaching him the art of archery and the ways of the forest.

However, Henry's life had been marked by loss and disappointment. His father had passed away when he was young, leaving him with only a book about Little Red Riding Hood as a reminder of their time together. His stepfather, a member of the Drunken Knights, was often absent or drunk, leaving Henry to fend for himself.

Henry's mother was a wise

medicine woman who had found a way to make life with a twist. She lived in a house carved out of a giant Redwood tree, symbolizing her connection to the forest and its secrets.

Despite his challenges, Henry had found a deep connection to the land and its inhabitants. He had learned there was still beauty and wonder, even in the face of loss and hardship. And he knew that he would always be a part of this magical world, surrounded by the majesty of the forest and the kindness of its people.

Henry's story reminds us that life is full of joy and sorrow and that we can find beauty and connection even in the darkest times.

On rare days when it rained or was chilly, you could find Redwood tucked away in his bedroom, the highest room in the tree house. He would be reading his books; the pages inked mined by candlelight.

Cooking routine windy reminds you Henry sought shelter and comfort in his favorite spot with a warm and cozy blanket on a cold and windy day. As he turned the pages of his favorite book, the flickering candlelight cast a warm and inviting glow, providing a sense of security and calm. Though the hours passed quickly, Henry savored every moment, finding solace in the familiar story.

Henry opened his eyes as the morning light broke through the window and found himself in a quiet, dark room. The candle had burned out, marking the end of another night spent alone. Despite his loneliness,

Henry got up from his chair and went to the kitchen, determined to find solace in the familiar cooking routine.

Looking out the window, he saw a fawn grazing lazily on the lush green grass outside. Though the sight was beautiful, it only reminded him of his isolation. As he harvested the mushrooms, the earthy and spicy smell overwhelmed him, causing him to feel dizzy and disoriented. Despite the warning signs, he persevered, driven by determination and a desire to create something delicious.

Ultimately, his efforts were rewarded with a warm and hearty soup that filled him with comfort and satisfaction. Though the journey had been burdensome, Henry knew he was not alone. Each day came new opportunities to connect with the world and find joy in the little things. And though the path ahead might be uncertain, he took comfort in knowing he was not alone in his struggles. Nearby, Robin and his merry men searched for that fawn to reunite it with its mother. R in and his men tracked the fawn, which had led them to the Jr. family's home.

As Robin and his team approached the house, they were on high alert, ready to respond to emergencies. As he drew closer, Robin's attention was caught by a tiny, trembling fawn in the grass. He cradled the vulnerable creature gently, feeling its heartbeat against his chest.

But as he held the fawn, Robin's sharp eyes noticed something else in the grass. It was his dear friend, Henry, lying still and silent. Robin rushed over to him, his heart aching as he realized Henry had eaten a poisonous mushroom.

With profound empathy, Robin gathered Henry and carried him to safety. He placed him in a glass coffin with care, watching over him with a heavy heart. His friend's welfare was his only concern.

As he waited, Robin felt the weight of his friend's body against his own. He could see the lines of pain etched on Henry's face, and he felt a deep sorrow for what his friend was going through. He knew he would stay by Henry's side, no matter how long it took, for he was a true friend.

And so, Robin waited, his eyes fixed on his friend's face. He knew that he had done everything he could, but he also knew he would be there for Henry, no matter what. Robin was a kind and empathetic soul who would always be there for those in need.

Chapter Sixteen

WRITTEN IN STONES

The Dumpling Coin was a place that was not just

beautiful and elegant but also deeply empathetic. Its name was inspired by the crumbling brick wall of Humpty's Fallen Wall, and it was situated near the Swamps of Morrow. The people who visited the Dumpling Coin were there for the exquisite silk the hanging willow vines produced and the warmth and hospitality of the caretakers who called it home.

The fashion tailors at the Dumpling Coin, Anabelle, Melody, and Darla, were known for their exquisite fashion sense and empathetic nature.

They understood that beauty and elegance were not just a matter of appearance but also the heart. They ensured that everyone who visited the Dumpling Coin felt welcomed and valued.

The Littles and their family, who were the caretakers of the Dumpling Coin, were also profoundly empathetic. They understood that the beauty of the hanging willow vines and the mossy brick walls were not just for show but also for comfort. They ensured the clubhouse was where families and friends could gather and solace in the beautiful surroundings.

In summary, the Dumpling Coin was a place of beauty, elegance, and empathy. It was a reminder that true beauty comes not just from outward appearance but also from the heart. The people who called the Dumpling Coin home understood this deeply, and they ensured that everyone who visited felt welcomed, valued, and comforted.

Juliet was a bright, imaginative, and curious young girl who spent most of her days lost in a world of wonder and magic. Her love for books was insatiable, and she could often be found lost in the pages of her favorite stories, turning each page with bated breath as she journeyed with the characters through the fantastical worlds they inhabited.

When Juliet wasn't reading, she loved to explore the nearby swamp forest, where she would spend hours lost in thought, pondering the mysteries of the natural world around her. She reveled in the forest's peace, where she could be alone with

her thoughts and let her imagination run wild.

Despite being an only child with
busy parents, Juliet never felt
lonely, for her mind was always
brimming with ideas, and her
imagination was her constant
companion. She had created a
world where anything was possible, and she could be whoever
she wanted.

One evening, just before dusk,
Juliet retreated to her little corner of the world, a makeshift
tent fashioned from tattered
clothes. She lit candles through-

out the room, casting a soft and warm glow. As she opened her favorite book, Little Red Riding Hood, she felt herself transported into the story, walking hand in hand with the brave and adventurous protagonist.

The story filled Juliet with a sense of wonder and excitement, inspiring her to be brave and curious in her own life. She felt a surge of energy and creativity coursing through her veins, and she knew that there was so much more to discover and learn in the world around her.

As she reached the book's final pages, Juliet felt a sense of joy and fulfillment and a hint of sadness, knowing that the story would soon end. But she knew that the end of one story was just the beginning of another, and she was excited to see what new adventures lay ahead of her. Juliet closed the book and smiled, grateful for the gift of imagination and inspiration that books brought into her life.

As Juliet woke up the day after she arrived in the swampy woods, she felt a sense of cu-

riosity and excitement. The unknown was calling her, and
she couldn't resist its pull. She
wondered what lay beyond the
stretch of swampy woods and
where it might lead her.

As she skipped through the
swamp, she could feel the mud
squishing between her toes
and the humid air filling her
lungs. Despite the discomfort,
she was determined to explore
the world around her and satis-
fy her sense of adventure.

She hesitated momentarily
when she came across a trail

leading into the woods. But her desire to explore and discover new things overruled her doubts, and she stepped onto the path, ready for whatever lay ahead.

She felt like she was entering a different realm in the woods. The trees towered over her, casting long shadows on the forest floor. It was beautiful and intimidating, but Juliet didn't let her fear stop her from moving forward.

When she came across the signs pointing in different directions, she felt a sense of uncertainty. Which path should she take? She explored the area around the signs, hoping that something would guide her.

As she looked up at the trees, she noticed something sparkling in the branches of a hidden tree. It was a glass coffin with a boy dressed in red lying inside. Juliet was amazed by sight. She felt like she had stumbled upon something magical and mysterious.

As she pounded on the glass, she felt a sense of empathy for the boy inside. She wondered what had happened to him and how he ended up in the coffin. She thought about the power of love and the importance of human connection. She felt connected to the boy, even though she knew nothing about him.

As she turned to leave, she felt like the forest was alive with magic and wonder. She knew there was still so much to explore and discover, and she felt grateful for the opportunity to experience it all.

CHAPTER SEVENTEEN

CHARLOTTE'S FARM

Papa Wilbur is a skilled house painter from the

beautiful state of Maryland. In addition to his painting expertise, he also holds the prestigious position of a royal skipper. Papa Wilbur's passion for art was ignited during his days of painting people's homes for a meager wage of one penny a day. Despite facing financial hardships and being a tired older man, he never gave up on his dreams and continued to pursue his passion for art. Eventually, his hard work paid off, and he became a successful artist, inspiring many others to follow their dreams despite the odds.

After the sun went down, he had his wife and two daughters to keep him company. Papa Wilbur had a wise but dreamy mind; he had wished for more things for a simple lifestyle, a dream about the extraordinary wonders and what it might be like if he was a little bit upside down, dreams where only they could come true, he thought.

As the sun began to set, casting a warm orange glow across the sky, Debby quietly crept past her sister Becky's bedroom, taking extra care not to wake her. She made her way to the old ladder leading up to the dusty attic space of her family home. With each creaking step, Debby's excitement grew, knowing that her favorite books and a place of solitude awaited her in the attic.

When she finally reached the top, she could see the dust particles illuminated by the flickering light of the candle she had brought with her. The candle sat atop an old wooden crate, casting a warm, cozy glow on the rough wooden walls of the attic. The space was filled with the familiar musty smell of old books, and Debby felt immediately at home.

She settled into the dinky old rocker chair, feeling the rough, worn fabric of the cushion against her skin. She picked up her favorite book, Charlotte's Web, and began reading about Wilbur the Pig's adventures and his friend, Charlotte the Spider. Debby found it amusing that the pig was named after her father and the spider after her grandmother. She loved how E .B. White blended reality with fantasy, creating a world where animals could talk and go on adventures just like people.

As she read, the story came to life, and she felt like she was right there on the farm with Wilbur and Charlotte. She could feel the sun's warmth on her face and the cool breeze blowing through her hair. She could hear the sounds of the animals and smell the sweet scent of hay in the air.

Debby lost track of time as she read; before she knew it, the candle had burned to its last flicker. She closed the book and blew out the candle, feeling a sense of contentment wash over her. She knew she would always treasure these moments spent in the cozy attic, lost in the world of her favorite books.

The first light of dawn was starting to peek over the horizon, casting a warm, orange glow over the small town of Wilbur. The air was still and quiet, with only the distant chirping of birds breaking the silence. Amid this peaceful morning, the doorbell rang at Wilbur's family home, jolting Mama Teacup awake from her slumber.

As she stumbled to the door, rubbing the sleep from her eyes, Mama Teacup couldn't help but wonder who could be visiting so early in the morning. She swung the door open to find a box filled with hay and a giant pig with a bow around its neck on the doorstep. The unexpected gift took away Mama Teacup, and she brought the pig inside, setting it on the kitchen counter with a loud thud that shook the house.

As Mama Teacup contemplated what to do with the pig, she noticed something odd. The pig seemed to be in labor, and before she knew it, five tiny piglets were born, causing chaos in the kitchen as they scurried around on the slippery floor. Mama Teacup's heart was filled with wonder and amazement as she watched the piglets run around, their tiny bodies covered in soft, pink fur. They were the cutest things she had ever seen, and she couldn't help but smile at their adorable antics.

However, a sudden wave of fear soon interrupted Mama

Teacup's moment of joy. She realized she had no idea how to handle this situation and reached for a butcher knife from the kitchen drawer. But before she could move, the piglets moved in unison, their tiny bodies swaying rhythmically to a tune they could only hear.

Mama Teacup was amazed by the sight, and she couldn't help but laugh at the adorableness of it all. The piglets had transformed from a source of fear to a source of joy, and the entire family was laughing and clapping along to their perfor-mance. The kitchen was alive with their tiny squeals and laughter, and it was a moment that Mama Teacup would never forget.

And with that, Wilbur's family became known as "Mr. Wilbur's Pigs," a name that would stick with them forever. The piglets would grow up to be a beloved part of the family, and their im-promptu performance would go down in history as one of the most heartwarming moments in Maryland. Mama Teacup re-alized that even amid chaos and uncertainty, there was always room for joy and laughter, and she was grateful for the unexpected gift that had brought her family together uniquely.

CHAPTER
EIGHTEEN

TROUBLE
TROUT
SOUP

It's no secret that Tom Butler was a bit of a troublemak-

er in the small town of Maryland. At fifteen years old, he was a constant source of frustration for the school authorities and an annoyance to his classmates. But despite his mischievous ways, it was clear that Tom had a good heart.

Tom's closest friend was Huck Sawyer, and the two of them were always up to something. They would often get into trouble together but never meant any harm. They were looking for some excitement in their otherwise mundane lives.

Tom's rough and fun-loving nature often landed him in hot water, but he never let it get him down. He was always ready for the next adventure, and his carefree attitude was infectious. Even though he caused his fair share of problems, people couldn't help but love him.

It's important to remember that Tom was just a kid trying to find his place in the world. He didn't mean to cause trouble; it seemed to follow him wherever he went. Despite his reputation, he was still a beloved community member, and people were willing to forgive him for his misdeeds.

After the tragic loss of his mother, Tom had to leave his old life behind and his brother like friend and move to his Aunt Molly's farm. The farm was situated in a remote and mysterious area beyond the Shoe Inn, and to get to it, Tom had to cross the Huntsmen Woods. As he entered the woods, he felt a deep sense of unease, as if the silence surrounding him was alive and waiting to swallow him whole. The woods were surrounded by elaborate hedge gardens filled with winding paths and intricate designs that seemed to lead to nowhere.

As Tom approached the farm, he couldn't help but notice its sorry state. The once beautiful farmhouse was now run-down and neglected, with peeling paint, cracked and broken windows, and a roof that leaked in several places. Despite its dilapidated condition, Aunt Molly's farm had a certain rustic charm that caught Tom's attention. Vast fields surrounded the farm, and the air was filled with the sweet scent of wildflowers and the gentle sound of bird-song.

However, it didn't take Tom long to realize this was no ordinary home. The Maryland Asylum was a unique residence that housed physically or mentally challenged children. Tom was introduced to a diverse group of children, each with unique stories and struggles. Some used wheelchairs, while others had severe developmental disorders or mental illnesses.

Despite the challenges, Tom was determined to make the most of his new life. He spent his days exploring the vast property, tending to the farm animals, and getting to know his new companions. He was fascinated by their different personalities, and he was always there to help them when they needed him. Although the future was uncertain, Tom couldn't help but feel a sense of curiosity and wonder about what lay ahead. He knew he had found a new home and was ready to embrace all the adventures that awaited him.

Tom's heart was racing as he approached Aunt Molly's farmhouse. He had heard so much about the peculiar children who lived there and couldn't wait to meet them. The old, rustic farmhouse looked like it had seen better days but had a certain charm that Tom couldn't ignore. As he walked through the creaky wooden door, he was hit with a musty smell that made him wrinkle his nose. "Hello?" he called out tentatively, but there was no response.

As he explored the house, Tom couldn't help but feel a sense of awe and wonder at the history surrounding him. The walls were lined with old photographs and paintings, and the furniture was a mixture of antique and modern pieces. As he went up the stairs to his new room, he could hear the floorboards creaking beneath his feet. It was like the house was alive and had a story to tell.

Finally, he reached his room and opened the door. Inside, there was a small bed, a dresser, and a desk. The room was sparsely furnished, but it was clean and tidy. As he put his bag down, he felt a sense of excitement mixed with apprehension. He knew his role as the children's new caretaker would be complex, but he was determined to do his best. He had high hopes that he could positively impact their lives and give them the care and attention they deserved.

Tom had always been curious, constantly seeking adventure and excitement daily. However, it wasn't until he stumbled upon a forgotten library in the mansion home of his Aunt Molly's asylum that he genuinely found what he was looking for. The library was hidden away in a small attic space, and as soon as Tom entered the room, he was struck by the musty smell and dimly lit atmosphere.

Rows upon rows of dusty books filled the shelves, the titles and covers of which were intriguing and mysterious. Tom couldn't resist the urge to explore the collection, his fingers tracing over the spines of the books as he made his way through the room. His eyes landed on a set of books that piqued his interest - mystery and adventure novels that promised thrilling tales of suspense and danger.

Tom eagerly grabbed one of the books and settled into a cozy corner of the room, the pages crackling as he flipped through them. As he read, he was transported to different worlds, vicariously through the characters and experiencing a thrill he had never felt before. The books were filled with inked pages describing vividly the adventures and mischief Tom had always dreamed of experiencing. It was as if the books had been written specifically for him, tailored to his every desire.

Tom was hooked. He devoured book after book, losing himself in the stories and reliving some of his fondest memories. The discovery of the library had sparked a passion in him that he had never known before, and he knew that he would continue to seek out new books and new adventures for years to come.

As the storm raged outside, Tom sought refuge in the library of lost books. The sound of thunder was deafening, and every flash of lightning illuminated the room, casting an eerie glow on the shelves of forgotten books. The musty smell of old paper filled the air, and rain tapping on the windowpanes provided soothing background noise. After a long day of caretaking, Tom was looking for an escape, and he found it in The Secret Garden, which he had picked out from the shelves.

The book was a masterpiece, and every page was a treat. The story transported him to a world of wonder and magic, where the beauty of nature was celebrated and every soul was capable of transformation. The vivid descriptions of flowers, trees, and gardens filled Tom's mind with colorful images, and the characters in the story were so accurate that he felt like he was living among them. The world of The Secret Garden was a stark contrast to life at the Maryland Asylum, where everything was dull and gray. But in the pages of this book, Tom found a garden of solace and hope, where he could escape from the harsh reality of his everyday life.

The first rays of the morning sun had just risen, casting a warm and inviting glow across every room in the massive mansion. The soft light filtering through the expansive windows illuminated the tall attic space. Tom, however, found himself still wide awake, lost in thought about the book he had read the previous night and the few pages he had finished. The narrative had left him wondering if the hedges of the mazes outside had any secret passages tucked away within their walls.

Determined to find out, Tom quickly got dressed for the day, being careful not to wake his Aunt Molly, who would undoubtedly have a long list of chores for him. With a sense of adventure, he carefully snuck into the courtyard and headed straight for the hedge mazes.

As he scoured the scattered hedge maze, he found himself in an archway that led to a hidden pathway. Tom was excited as he followed the trail, hoping it would lead him to a secret garden like the one he had read about the night before. His heart raced as he explored the garden, and his excitement grew as he stopped to look around. Sure enough, he smiled and whispered to himself, "A secret garden, I knew it!"

But his joy was short-lived as he turned to the right and was shocked to discover oddly painted white roses. Out of the corner of his eye, he saw a deck of card-looking soldiers, a boy in a red hood, a girl in a pink dress and a red bow, singing away while carrying a bucket full of red paint. They repeatedly painted the white roses red while singing in a melodic tune, "We are painting the roses red; we are painting roses red."

This strange sight took Tom aback. He ran back, wondering what he had just walked into and what it all meant. As he pondered, he couldn't help but question himself about the curious encounter and its meaning.

.

.

CHAPTER NINETEEN

NOTRE HUNCHBACK WISHING

N estled between the Cap-
tain's family blacksmith

shop was the humble abode of the Ginger Family in Maryland Square. The Gingers were modest folks who, despite not being wealthy, found joy in their simple way of life. They yearned to share their happiness with a little boy or girl and often talked about adopting a child to bring more love and warmth to their home.

Despite their struggles, the Gingers never hesitated to help their neighbors. They were always willing to lend a hand to anyone in need. Their kindness and generosity were well-known throughout the town and held a special place in people's hearts.

The Gingers' selflessness and concern for others made them an integral part of the community. They were admired and respected by everyone around them. Adopting a child to share their love and joy reflected their empathetic and caring nature.

It's heartwarming to see people like the Gingers who put others first, even in their struggles. They remind us that there is always kindness and love in the world and that we can all make a difference in someone's life.

The day was full of promise as Mr. and Mrs. Ginger set out to clean the Dumpling Soup orphanage. They were a kind-hearted couple who knew the value of hard work and were determined to make ends meet. As they began their tasks, Mr. Ginger started repairing a section of the outside garden while Mrs. Ginger went to the children's room to start cleaning it up.

While cleaning, she heard a

small voice from the end of the bed seating. She saw a little boy sitting on the bench alone, reading a book. She could see that he was wearing a striped turtleneck and had a slight hunchback. Mrs. Ginger greeted him warmly and asked him about the book he was reading. However, the boy didn't respond.

Mrs. Ginger sat down next to him, and as she looked into his eyes, she could sense his fear and apprehension. She knew he had been dealt an intricate hand in life and deeply empathized with him. She wanted him to see that he was valued and loved, regardless of appearance.

Suddenly, the little boy, Hugo, ran off before Mrs. Ginger could see his face. She noticed his hunchback as he left, and her heart filled with compassion for the little boy. She followed him and stood beside him, wanting to show him she wasn't afraid of him.

Then, she saw his face, and his beauty struck her. She could see the pain and sadness in his eyes, and she knew that he needed someone to love and care for him. The soft light from the candle flickered, and she felt a deep connection with him then.

Hugo looked back at her and shyly smiled. He said, "Hi." Mrs. Ginger felt a rush of warmth and kindness flood her, and she knew she had found a new friend in Hugo. She promised herself that she would do everything in her power to make him feel loved and valued, and she knew that with her help, he could overcome any obstacle that life threw his way.

CHAPTER TWENTY

KETTLES LAMPS

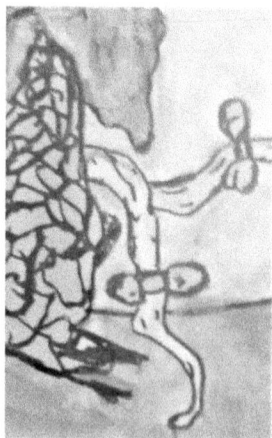

R umple Stine is a small, wiry
boy with tousled brown

hair and a sun-kissed complexion who lives on the outskirts of Maryland. He spends most of his days wandering the wilderness, exploring the dense forests, and playing with the animals that call it home. He has a deep connection with the natural world, and the creatures seem to sense his kind spirit, often approaching him without fear.

Despite his friendly nature, Rumple Stine is not well-liked by the townspeople of Maryland. He is known to be a thief, and his reputation has suffered. Whenever merchants come to town, he can lurk around the marking square, deftly grabbing whatever he can before disappearing into the woods. His actions have caused anger and frustration among the locals, who see him as a menace to their way of life.

Suzie Loe's story is a tragic one. She was just a young child when she got lost in the forest, stumbling upon an old beggar woman who took her in. The woman was initially kind but soon revealed herself to be cruel and manipulative. She locked Suzie away in a tower hidden deep in the Pine Woods, where she had been held captive for years. The tower is cold and damp, with little light and even less comfort. Suzie spends most of her days peering out the small window, dreaming of the day she will be rescued from prison.

Despite her dire circumstances, Suzie remains hopeful. She spends her time reading books that the older woman occasionally brings her, learning about the outside world and imagining what it would be like to live freely. She dreams of being rescued by a nobleman on a white steed, who will whisk her away to a better life under the stars.

The story begins with a scene of a quaint town where a traveling merchant is about to visit. The city is excited as the merchant is known to bring unique and rare items for trade. Among the residents is a young man named Rumple Stine, who is out collecting blackberries in the Pine Woods when he stumbles upon a towering stone structure. He is immediately captivated by the sight of it and hears the most beautiful singing coming from above.

As he hides behind a bush, he sees an old hooded woman approach the tower. She calls Suzie Loe inside the building, asking her to let down her pigtails. To Rumple's astonishment, the pigtails drop from the tower, and the older woman quickly climbs the stone walls.

Rumple climbs the tower to see the mysterious girl with the long pigtails and the enchanting voice. The next day, he discusses his plan with his best friend, Bamboo the Bear, while they continue to gather blackberries. Bamboo tells him about a magic bottle that traveling merchants have, which grants wishes to whoever possesses it on the nights of the golden moon.

Meanwhile, an old beggar woman travels through the Pine Woods mist to Suzie Loe's tower to see what her child needs and wants. It is clear that something magical and life-changing is about to happen to all these characters, and their lives will never be the same again.

The Buttermilk family's merchants had set up their vibrant and colorful stalls around the bustling town square. The air was filled with the aroma of freshly baked bread, roasted nuts, and exotic spices. Amidst the hustle and bustle, Rumple patiently waited for the golden full moon to rise. He had spent countless hours spinning the finest golden yarn from his mother's old spinning wheel, hoping to trade it for a magical bottle.

As the night before, Suzie Loe was lost in the Tales of The Arabian Nights pages, reading by candlelight in her tower. The flickering candlelight cast shadows on the pages of her book, and the stillness of the night was broken only by the sound of the crickets outside. As she turned the page, Suzie noticed a glimmer of light and looked up to see a string of gold hovering in the air. Mystified, she followed the string with her fingers, and as she touched it, a burst of magic emanated from her, lifting the string even higher into the sky.

Rumple arrived at the Buttermilk family's stall the following day, displaying his golden yarn. The Buttermilk family was impressed by his work's sheer beauty and quality and readily agreed to trade the yarn for the magical bottle. The golden yarn was a work of art - fine and delicate, with the lustrous sheen of silk. It was evident that Rumple had put his heart and soul into spinning this yarn.

Rumple rode off into the forest, his trusty panther at his side, feeling invigorated and purposeful. As he rode, he called out to Suzie Loe, whom he believed he was destined to rescue. "Suzie Loe, oh Suzie Loe, it's I, your rescuer. Let down your pigtails," he yelled with determination, his heart beating with excitement for the adventures that awaited him.

CHAPTER TWENTY-ONE

POTS AND PANS

Excellent In the heart of a
serene countryside, nes-

tled atop the rolling hills of Jack and Jill Hilltops, there is a small log cabin called Little House that serves as a home to a bright and imaginative six-and-a-half-year-old girl named Amy. Amy is the oldest of three daughters in this small pioneer family and dreams of new adventures.

Amy's father built the cabin with his hands, carefully harvesting and cutting nearby trees to create a warm and cozy abode for his family. Amy's mother is a devoted caretaker who cares for her daughters and ensures they are always happy and healthy.

Despite her family's love and attention, Amy often feels lonely as she doesn't have many friends, given the age difference between her and her sisters. However, she has found solace in the company of her handmade rag-stuffed animals, which her mother lovingly creates for her every year as a special birthday present.

Living in isolation can be challenging, but Amy's family has found happiness in their simple yet fulfilling life on Jack and Jill Hilltops. As an empathetic assistant, I understand how Amy may feel and hope she will continue to find joy in her imaginative mind and her small yet loving family.

The warm summer breeze gently rustled the blades of grass in the small prairie, where Amy sat playing with her favorite stuffed animal. The patchwork of old rags and animal parts sewn together by her papa had always been a source of comfort and joy for her. As she played with her beloved friend,

Amy's imagination ran wild, inventing stories about the wonders of nature and the magical world surrounding her.

Amy had created a make-believe world where everything had a unique personality and charm. She had built tiny homes for her stuffed animal friends - Whinnies, Hoglet, and Jack - each with its name and story. The World of Pooh, her mother's favorite book, had inspired her to create new characters and adventures in her imaginary world.

As much as she enjoyed her make-believe world, Amy sometimes wished that her friends were alive to share in the joy of her imaginary world. Her wild vision often took her beyond the boundaries of her imagination, and she longed for her friends to be there with her, exploring the small prairie and discovering its wonders.

Amy's dreams were filled with hopes of her friends coming to life one day, and she poured her heart into her imaginative world, hoping that her fervent wishes would come true. The small prairie was her sanctuary; her stuffed animals were her cherished companions, providing comfort and solace when the world felt too overwhelming.

The small log cabin that was her childhood home was filled with warmth, love, and comfort. As she carefully climbed up the old, rocky ladder one night, she felt a sense of peace and tranquility. She knew that she was safe and secure in her little log cabin, surrounded by the love of her family.

As she began to read, the flickering candlelight illuminated the pages of her favorite book, and the sound of raindrops tapping on the rooftop was a soothing lullaby that accompanied her through the night. A powerful storm raged outside, and Amy felt a twinge of fear, but she knew she was not alone. Her family was nearby, and they would keep her safe from harm.

The following day, the smell of pancakes sizzling on the pan woke her up, and she eagerly sat down at the small wooden table. Her mother had already set out a plate of pancakes, each smothered with delicious fresh maple syrup from their maple tree. She felt grateful for the love and care that her mother had put into making the breakfast. However, as she finished eating, she remembered her stuffed animal friends in her wooded play community, and a sense of guilt washed over her.

Scared and afraid of finding them in ruins, she rushed directly to her spot on the hundred acres. As she emerged from the woods, she saw her stuffed friends running in the sunshine, happy and content. She felt a sense of empathy for them, realizing that they could be satisfied without her. She spent the rest of the morning with them, describing tales and tales, and later, she went back to her small log cabin with a sense of fulfillment and contentment, knowing that she had made a difference in the lives of her stuffed friends.

CHAPTER TWENTY-TWO

LITTLE YAMS

Nestled amidst the rolling hills on Cherry Lane is the picturesque Baa Baa Black

Sheep Farm, owned and operated by Little Berry Thumb and his Auntie Bow Peep. They are known throughout Maryland for producing the most excellent wool anyone has seen or touched. The wool is so delicate and soft that it feels like a cloud.

One sunny day, Berry and his best friend, The Little Black Sheep, made their way to the lively town square with wool bundles for sale. The town was bustling with people, and everyone eagerly awaited the next wool sale, knowing they would receive the best quality wool. It was the perfect opportunity to buy wool to create the most exquisite clothing.

The townsfolk marveled at the wool as Berry and his sheep proudly displayed their beautiful wares in the courtyard's center at noon. The quality of the wool was unmatched, and everyone was willing to pay a premium price of two gold coins for just a piece.

Berry was living a life he had always dreamed of, but little did he know that one night would change his life forever. He found himself sitting in the attic, a dimly lit space filled with old and dusty furniture, where he was enjoying a warm slice of delicious plum pie. However, his enjoyment was short-lived, as he was constantly haunted by the thought of being caught and punished for eating his auntie's pie. He glanced around the room to take his mind off it and noticed a small pile of old books in the corner. Curiosity got the better of him, and he walked over to examine the pile. As he lifted the first book, he noticed the title "The

Life and Adventures of Robinson Crusoe." Berry had heard of this book before but had never read it, so he tried it.

As Berry Thumb started reading, he felt himself drawn into the story, lost in its intricate details and vivid descriptions. The book was so fascinating that he forgot about the pie and the punishment awaiting him. The only light source was a single candlestick flickering in the drafty room, but Berry was too absorbed in the story to notice.

As he read on, he felt himself

being transported into another world filled with danger and adventure. He could almost smell the salty sea air and feel the salty spray of the ocean as the story progressed. But as the candle burned to its last flicker, Berry finished the last bite of his pie and reluctantly put the book down. He felt a sense of loss like he was leaving behind a world he had grown to love.

But before he could process his thoughts, he was thrown into a world of his imagination, which was terrifying and exhilarating. He found himself on a rickety raft, adrift in the vast ocean with nothing but the stars to guide him. Fear crept over him as he realized he was alone and lost, without knowing how he got there or what lay ahead.

As he landed on the island, he was in awe of the natural beauty surrounding him. But his sense of wonder was short-lived as he realized he was not alone on the island. A tribe of cannibals was chasing him, their eyes filled with hunger and rage. Berry ran for his life, dodging spears and pitchforks, his heart pounding with fear. It was a close call, but he managed to escape with the help of a newfound companion named Freddy.

As they sailed away, Berry couldn't help but feel a sense of empathy for the characters in the book he had just read. He had been thrown into a world of danger and excitement, with nothing but his wits and courage to guide him. It was a world that he had never imagined but one that he would never forget.

PART 3
CHARMING
CURSED

CHAPTER TWENTY-THREE

BUTTER AND BREAD

Nestled in a peaceful cor-ner of South Avenue, Maryland, stand two homes that emanate warmth and comfort, home to two wealthy families with their maiden and bulter serving them. The first house is home to the Wickers family, with a graceful maiden whose beauty is only matched by her kindness and humility. Across the street is a second house, where a diligent butler resides and home to the Potters family.

Despite living in separate houses, they can see each other's rooflines, adding to the picturesque view of the street. Notably, the maiden and butler were employed by two illustrious families of their time: Wickers and Potters. Rozella Glass and Prince Charming were highly skilled at their jobs, serving as house cleaners and food preparers for their wealthy families.

The Rozella Glass was known for her exceptional cleaning skills, which left the Wickers household shining like a diamond. Her dedication to her duties was admirable, but the family she served didn't love her. On the other hand, Prince Charming was remarkable in his food preparation skills. He had a knack for creating mouth-watering delicacies that left the Potters family licking their fingers; however, unlike Rozella Glass, Prince Charming was loved by the Potter family.

During their breaks, Rozella Glass and Prince Charming often found solace in each other's company. As they gazed out of the large, round windows of the family home they served, they would share moments of quiet reflection, lost in their thoughts and feelings.

They often thought of each other in those fleeting moments, feeling deeply empathetic and understanding that only they could share. Their hearts would fill with an all-encompassing love that they couldn't help but embrace, and they would find themselves lost in the possibilities of a future together.

As they stood together, side by side, they would share stories of their lives, laughing and smiling, feeling a sense of connection that could not be broken. They knew they were not alone in those moments and had found someone who truly cared.

The Wickers sisters were Rose, Beatrice, and Martha Wicker. Martha and Beatrice are the nasty, ugly twins named by their sister Rose for their rude behavior and illogical ways.

Rose was a shy and quiet little girl. She is always courteous, but she is pretty shy. Rose befriended the animals around her, such as the attic mice, earning their respect and liking. She also befriended Rozella, the housekeeper.

Still, most days, you'll find Rose reading along with her mother's old books to take her mind off the ugliness of her sisters, giving her a taste of happiness.

Rozella and Rose had bonded stronger than ever before, and it felt like they were sisters even though Rozella had worked for them for years.

Rose had discovered Rozella's secret crush on the butler next door, even if Rozella didn't show it. It came down to one night only when that love would rise on its own, perhaps with the help of childhood magic.

It was the night before the Townhouse dance ball for the wealthy, including their maidens or butlers. Rozella was ecstatic because she had cleaned the house extra lovely and tidy the day before. She hoped to have enough gold coins to buy a new dress she had been wearing for a month, but the harsh reality set in as the deadline approached.

Rose was in her spot inside that old attic that night, in the candlelight shining out to the moonlights, reading the

Cinderella story to a newborn mouse.

As night fell, the sparks sang out, touching a child's heart and lifting to the bright side colors of a rainbow. Bringing life excites everyone who has imagined becoming the wonders of stories, bringing out magic imagery.

Gift of a fairy godmother wish could see the stars that night as Rozella walked down the lighted candle streets and headed back home. Something more was brewing in the streets for the nights; dreams would come into existence.

A warmhearted touch could always return as a comforting gift. Rozella continued down the town's brick pathway until she arrived at the town square. At midnight, the clock tower struck twelve. Rozella paused to make a wish at the old well that surrounded the clock tower. True love was on her mind, not luck, but with wishes; anything is plausible, and anything can go wrong at any given take.

Rozella's gaze returned to the stars as she dropped her gold coin into the water well, which twinkled and sparkled. A star fell from the heavens and shot into Rozella's heart as the coin splashed at the bottom of the well. A Blue fairy, holding a wand inside her palms, her hands in gowned blues, stands, smiling with her wand.

"Dear child, I have watched you from the heavens," the fairy spooked as she continued to speak into her words, "your dearies; a daring woman of this age, so kind-hearted, warm, caring, a person who, no matter what or where you go, there is always warmth so the night is a night to give you a gift for your gift of heart-wanting dreams."

Rozella stood there, wondering what the blue fairy's words meant, but soon, her eyes and heart could see what good spirits could achieve with a wave of a wand and a touch of magic; Rozella gained the gift of love and beauty.

The gift she received was a gown she could fantasize about more than ever. Spinning around, watching it twirl, and with the fancy glass heels she wore, the blue fairy smile faded into the distance.

That night, there was a dance at the Townhouse Ball. Rozella wore her new dress and shoes at night with a peeking edge. She danced proudly and joined in the fun. That same spark of magic returned for Rozella, but this time, it was replaced by love. Rozella and Charming formed as lovers should. Rose collapsed in the catch; she was the blue fairy, and her mission had been completed.

CHAPTER TWENTY-FOUR

GLASS SLIPPER

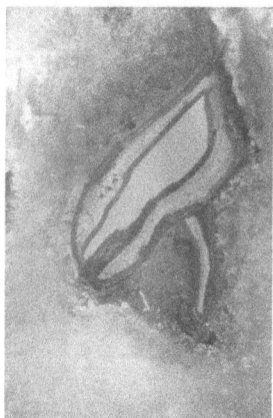

Rozella Glass and Prince Charming had grown tired of their glamorous life as maids and butlers to the wealthy. They craved a change and wanted to pursue their true passions. They decided to leave their jobs and move to a humble cottage on the town's outskirts.

Rozella Glass and Prince Charming had grown tired of their glamorous life as maids and butlers to the wealthy after marrying one another. Now, Rozzella Charming and her Husband, Prince Charming, were craving a change and wanted to pursue their true passions. They decided to leave their jobs and move to a humble cottage on the town's outskirts.

The cottage was a charming little abode with a thatched roof and a white picket fence. It was surrounded by tall trees and a lush garden home to various birds and butterflies. As they walked through the garden, they could hear the gentle rustle of the leaves and birds chirping.

 Inside the cottage was a cozy living room with a fireplace that kept them warm during the winter months. The walls were adorned with paintings they had created together, each telling a unique story. The kitchen was small but functional, and they enjoyed cooking meals together using fresh produce from the garden.

In their free time, they would sit on the porch and admire the beauty of the countryside. They often took long walks, sketching and writing down their ideas. Their passion for art and literature kept them motivated and inspired, and they spent many happy hours lost in their creative pursuits.

Though their life was simple, they were content. They had found a home where they could be themselves and pursue their dreams without distractions. The cottage had become a sanctuary where they could unleash their creativity and live a purposeful life.

Rozella and Prince Charming's journey was long and arduous, fraught with challenges and setbacks that tested their resolve and fortitude. From the beginning, they knew their path would not be easy, but they were determined to chase their dreams no matter what.

As they embarked on their journey, they encountered numerous obstacles threatening their plans. Financial struggles were a constant source of stress as they struggled to make ends meet while pursuing their creative passions. Rejections from publishers were also frequent, which could have easily demoralized them. However, they refused to give up and instead used these setbacks as fuel to propel them forward.

Through it all, Rozella and Prince Charming remained united in pursuing a shared dream. They found solace in each other's company and took comfort in the simple joys of life. Whether sharing a meal or walking in the park, they cherished every moment together.

Their unwavering courage and determination were remarkable, as they refused to let adversity defeat them. Despite seemingly insurmountable challenges, they remained optimistic that they would one day achieve their dreams. And in the end, their persistence paid off, as they achieved the success they had worked so hard for.

Now head their households the Charmings had their very own ballroom dance and art gallery at the townhouse were their dreams had just begun and at a peek and night one's heart and glass heels and a stolen heart beauty and one happy every after could be said and down, but the table of that happy ever after couldn't last forever if want to for Rozella Charming and Prince Charming. Darken times will rise, and happiness will come with deep sadness for them in upcoming months; Rozella Charming and Prince Charming's baby will be born, and the spark of the charming curse will raise its disheartening ways.

Sleeping Beauty Charming, the daughter of Rozzella Charming and Prince Charming, was born on Chrismas day, and anxiety and fear as tears flowed down both Charming's face for their baby girl was doomed to die and turn to nothing but ashes and dust on her sixteen birthday after pricking her finger on spinning wheel fell asleep for hundreds of years and awakening by true loves kiss.

Tears shedding, the Charmings had now mother and father to their newborn child, and her fate came one single tear hitting a white rose. In a spark of sparkling fairy dust, three tiny fairies appeared in kindness and pure hearts. They granted three wishes to the Charming daughter: three beautiful gifts, one of authentic beauty and grace, one of song, and lastly, a kiss of life for the child will prick her finger on a spinning wheel at sixteen but won't Shriver to dust by true love kiss but live happy after just like her mother and her mother did.

The time came just like it said the beauty had fallen asleep, and the old cottage of the charmings slept for hundreds of years in their humble cottage until their child had awoken in true love kiss.

PART 4
PRINCE
AND THE
FROG
PRINCESS

CHAPTER TWENTY-FIVE

A CUP A TEA

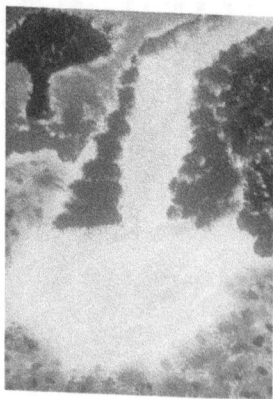

Tucked away in the corner of the quaint and serene Cherry Lane lies the charming abode of the Goldies, a family known for their warm hospitality and their unwavering commitment to nurturing the most exquisite blood cherries that grace the street. As you approach their house, you are greeted by the sight of the bountiful cherry trees lining the street in a vibrant red hue. The Goldies' home is an idyllic sanctuary surrounded by a colorful garden that boasts a delightful array of flowers.

The sweet aroma of cherries permeates the air, creating an inviting atmosphere that beckons you in. As you step inside, you are welcomed by the warm smiles of the Goldies, who take great pride in their cherries, which they tend to with love and care. They are the keepers of the most succulent and juicy cherries in town, and their reputation has spread far and wide, attracting cherry lovers from all over.

The Goldies are an integral part of the community, and their passion for cherries is infectious. They are always happy to share their knowledge and expertise with anyone interested, and their enthusiasm for their craft is truly inspiring. The blood cherries they cultivate are nothing short of a masterpiece, a testament to their hard work, dedication, and love for their craft.

Mr. Goldie was renowned throughout Maryland for his exceptional cherry-picking skills. He had spent years perfecting his craft, which showed in the quality of his work. The townspeople were immensely proud of their cherry harvest and had a reputation for producing the best cherries in the entire region. Mrs. Goldie, on the other hand, was equally celebrated for her exceptional tea brewing skills. Her cherry tea recipe was a well-kept secret, and it was believed to possess mystical powers. Many townfolks swore by its ability to bring wisdom and the gift of dreaming.

The Goldie family had a son named Cinder Goldie, a vibrant and imaginative young man. Despite his tendency to cause mischief, he was beloved by everyone in the town. Cinder had a natural talent for entertaining people with his jokes, games, and riddling tales. His wild imagination was inspired by the stories he read in the local bookstore, his family's attic, and his vast collection of fairy tale books. As Cinder matured, he gained more respect and admiration from the townspeople for his exceptional storytelling skills. Even Miss Pots, a school teacher, was enamored with Cinder's active imagination and used it to teach children about the value of creativity and fun.

Cinder's love for reading and storytelling continued to grow, and he spent every night regaling his family and friends with new tales. He was fascinated by the old stories he found in his family's attic and spent hours poring over them, trying to bring them to life. The townsfolk couldn't get enough of his humor and wit, and they would often gather around him, eager to hear his latest tales.

However, little did Cinder know that his life was about to change forever.

Cinder indulged in a delicious pot pie and refreshing root beer at the cozy and inviting Royalties Pub, a popular spot in town for locals and visitors alike. As he savored his meal, he couldn't help but eavesdrop on a group of people sharing an intriguing tale about a cursed princess and an evil fairy god-mother.

The storytellers consisted of some boisterous and inebriat-ed knights, an unsavory-look-ing older man, and an ostenta-tiously dressed man with long, flowing golden locks. Cinder listened intently as they discussed finding the lost King Adam and ending the curse on the land of Maryland. They also talked about a boy named William White, General Charming, and Eve, who played essential roles in the legend.

Cinder found the tale fascinating and pondered the possibility of it being confirmed. He couldn't help but wonder if the old fairytales were coming to life and if there was any truth to the legend. While most of the other patrons dismissed the story as mere fantasy, Cinder felt an urge to investigate further.

Sitting there, he realized that the cursed woods mentioned in the tale could be the dense pine tree forest beyond Cherry Lane. This forest had always given off a sinister and ominous vibe, and Cinder wondered if it could be the place where the lost princess was hidden.

Cinder set out on his adventure with a heavy backpack containing books, cookies, milk, and cheese. The woods were dense, and the trees towered over him, casting long shadows on the forest floor. The sunlight filtered through the leaves, creating a beautiful play of light and shadows.

As he journeyed more profoundly into the woods, he noticed a dense patch of misty fairy dust in the distance. He was curious and followed the trail that led him to an enchanting garden. The garden was filled with brightly colored flowers, and the scent of lavender and roses filled the air.

In the garden's center, he found an old, abandoned cottage. The cottage was made of wood and had a thatched roof that was covered in moss and vines. The door was slightly ajar, and its creaking sound as he pushed it open echoed through the silent woods.

As he entered the cottage, he was greeted by the sight of a cozy kitchen to his left. The kitchen had a wooden table with seven small stools and a sink with a rusty tap. To his right was the living room with a wooden grand piano and rustic cupboards. He noticed an old kettle pot beside a comfortable armchair that looked inviting.

As he looked around, he felt a sense of familiarity. It was as though he had read about a similar place before. He sat in the armchair and pulled out his backpack full of books. After flipping through each page, he found a picture of a cottage that looked just like the one he was in. He gasped when he realized that it was the cottage of Snow White and the Seven Dwarfs.

Excitedly, he ran up the stairs to the attic and found seven little beds with each of the dwarfs' names carved into them. The beds were small and made of wood, with little blankets and pillows. He felt a sense of wonder as he looked around, imagining the dwarves sleeping soundly in their beds.

His thoughts raced as he realized that the town he lived in was cursed and stuck in a fairytale from the 1600s. He was overwhelmed with excitement, knowing that the tales he had heard from the Drunken Knights were true. He felt a sense of adventure and determination, knowing that he had to uncover the truth and end the curse on Maryland once and for all.

CHAPTER TWENTY-SIX

SPELLBINDING KISS

As the sun slowly descended below the horizon, Cinder's gaze was drawn towards the enchanting garden and the seven dwarfs' cottage. The garden was a riot of colors, with vibrant flowers and lush greenery. The cottage, though small, was charming and inviting, with a well-worn path leading up to its door. Cinder felt an irresistible urge to explore every inch of this magical place, which seemed to hold so many secrets.

As he settled down on an old, creaky bed, he noticed a candle flickering on the nearby stairs. He lit it, and the warm, golden glow illuminated the room, casting a gentle warmth over everything. The room was simple, with rustic wooden furniture and a cozy fireplace. Cinder sat at the edge of the bed, his heart and mind racing as he lost himself in deep contemplation. He took out his favorite storybook, 'The Princess and the Frog,' and began to read. The words transported him to a world of magic and wonder, where anything was possible.

The magic of the place soon overtook him, and he drifted off to sleep. As he sleeps, the magic swirls around him, carrying him deeper into a dream world of enchantment. When he finally woke up, the first rays of dawn broke through the window, and he noticed that the candle's flames had dwindled to nothing but embers. He couldn't wait to explore the garden and cottage more, hoping to uncover the hidden secrets.

As he sat at the table, enjoying a simple breakfast of milk, cheese, and cookies, Cinder wondered where to find more secrets of this hidden and enchanting world. So, he set off to explore and found himself by a tranquil little pond. The pond was surrounded by tall trees, and the water was crystal clear. Cinder sat down by the pond's edge, lost in the peaceful allure of nature. He watched the ripples on the water's surface and listened to the gentle rustle of the leaves.

Suddenly, he heard a voice, and Cinder looked around, but nobody was there. He felt both frightened and curious as he paused to listen to the sounds of nature and the winds of the haunting, enchanting, magical world around him. Then,

he heard those tiny little voic-
es again and looking down, he
saw a frog sitting there. The
frog was unlike any Cinder had
ever seen before, its skin shimmering with an otherworldly
glow. Without any question, he
picked it up and kissed its
slimy lips. Suddenly, it sparkled
up, and enchanting fairy dust
and spellbinding ways twirled
around him.

Standing beside him was the
most enchanting and beautiful girl he had ever seen. She
had delicate features and long
hair that shone like gold. Cin-

der couldn't believe his eyes, but he knew she was real. They smiled at each other, and with a true love's kiss, their world was awakened, and the curse was finally broken. The garden and cottage were transformed into a magical wonderland, and Cinder and the girl lived happily ever after in this enchanted world.

Happy ever after as a time of old and cursed two worlds tale dreams wait!

Milton Keynes UK
Ingram Content Group UK Ltd.
UKHW030156051224
452010UK00010B/383